The Women's Press
science fiction

The Women's Press science fiction series features new titles by contemporary writers and reprints of classic works by well known authors. Our aim is to publish science fiction by women and about women; to present exciting and provocative feminist images of the future that will offer an alternative vision of science and technology, and challenge male domination of the science fiction tradition itself.

We hope that the series will encourage more women both to read and to write science fiction, and give the traditional science fiction readership a new and stimulating perspective.

JOSEPHINE SAXTON

Josephine Saxton was born in Halifax in 1935. She left school aged fifteen, was married twice, has four children and two grandchildren. Her works include *Queen of the States* (The Women's Press 1986) *The Hieros Gamos of Sam and An Smith, Vector for Seven, Group Feast*, a collection of stories under the title *The Power of Time* and many other stories in various anthologies over the years.

JOSEPHINE SAXTON

THE TRAVAILS OF JANE SAINT AND OTHER STORIES

The Women's Press

sf

First published in Great Britain by
The Women's Press Limited 1986
A member of the Namara Group
34 Great Sutton Street, London EC1V 0DX

British Library Cataloguing in Publication Data

Saxton, Josephine
    The travails of Jane Saint and other stories.
    I. Title
    823'.914[F]   PR6069.A96

    ISBN 0-7043-4037-2

Phototypeset by M.C. Typeset Limited, Chatham, Kent

Reproduced, printed and bound in Great Britain by
Hazell, Watson & Viney Ltd, Aylesbury, Bucks

For Roz Kaveney, Colin Greenland, Paul Kincaid, Mike Dickinson and all those who helped and encouraged me when I had given up.

A Plea to My Readers

This short preface springs from a deep fear of my own, with regard to the nature of my stories. If you believe that you are about to read some saga crossing Light Years, serious battles with futuristic weapons or androids who – but no, I do actually have androids somewhere in this collection, but, I think, with a difference – then you may be surprised. But I hope pleasantly. What I would really like is for *readers* to read my work, not only SF fans, who have, like rubber fetishists and gourmets, Special Tastes, and often cannot enjoy anything outside their label. Let me put in a plea, not just, as is sometimes necessary with Fantasy and Science Fiction, for a suspension of disbelief, but for a suspension of strictly labelled parameters. Then my deepest hope may be realised, which is that you will enjoy the stories for whatever they are.

Josephine Saxton
May 1986

Contents

Contents

The Travails of Jane Saint

This book is ten parts of the history of Jane Saint, Heroine of the Revolution, who journeyed in strange places and had adventures on her Quest. This is the true record of the beings she met and her travails along the way, and of what she endeavoured to accomplish for this world.

1. The One Tower

Jane Saint held out her arm for the tranquilliser. She did not want it but many things were now beyond her control. She hoped that she still had one chance left, and that her punishment here would enable her to make the most of it. She had been sentenced to total reprogramming, for the crime of being a revolutionary leader. The brainwashing would take place after several days in a sensory deprivation tank, designed to loosen all her normal associations. The input of approved ideas would easily take on a malleable self. The police doctors were chatting amiably one to another, the Spring sunshine illuminated them. An orderly spoke to Jane.

'I must say you are calm, usually they kick up a fuss, especially you female liberation types . . .' She put him to silence with her grey-eyed contempt, shrivelling him with silent disgust at his glib labelling. She did not want to waste energy screaming at these pigs, she had work to do. This treatment they were giving her could be ideal for her purpose, She intended to use it to obtain maximum concentration on her techniques for leaving her body behind. She planned to travel to the other world (if such there really was) and continue her work for the cause. Perhaps she could get other powers to intercede. She would need as much of herself and her memory as possible to go through with her, she did not want to trip off into some useless dreamland. There was no way of knowing whether her trial experiments had been delusion or not, but she had to try, and seriously. A true believer never gives up, and what else could she do in this situation?

She composed herself once more, trying to ignore the effect of the tranquilliser. Now the breathing, the counting, the mental picturing, everything she had been able to find out about this procedure she now tried, suppressing her own scepticism. She was determined they would not destroy her and her work, her hopes, her efforts to make a better world.

Her three children, her Melanie, Dolores and Sybil, they too were somewhere in this place they called a hospital. They also were preparing like their mother, they too were trying to survive in a killing world. They had been judged contaminated by their mother's ideas and therefore in need of care and protection. She sent them a mental message: 'Mother's coming soon' and that was all she had time for before they manacled her to the bottom of the tank so beautifully fashioned in solid glass. She felt the water seeping, at blood heat, creeping, up to her ears, lapping her lifted chin. Things could not be better, for she would be in a womb, an amniotic space-ship. They drew the blinds close, they left a little light while they put the lid over the vision of her red hair streaming like blood, needing flowers to be Ophelia. Then darkness, utter silence.

'This is it, Jane,' she told herself. 'Now, you will either get "through" and accomplish something important, or you will lose everything and never be yourself again.'

Down she went into the heights.

Jane Saint had everything she knew of to ensure a memory, but she had no notion of where and why she was. A telephone box ahead on the lonely moor. She decided to use it to ascertain her whereabouts, thinking that she must have had an accident, become dazed. There was no habitation in this windswept world of peatbogs, the only relief was an upheaving of rock, a sky on the move, racked yet determined not to reveal any secret; a Brontë land smeared with puce spewings of *Erica*, torsioned bonsai.

On the floor of the telephone box was a small blue nylon rucksack. Better not touch it, might contain a bomb.

Eventually the operator answered, and after much argument, stating that it was against the rules, told Jane that further up the path there was shelter. She was in Glun Cloud, which was not famous. Well then, sincere thanks.

The rucksack was a temptation. Not all abandoned packages contain bombs, some contain useful objects and food. Jane had nothing with her at all except the inexplicably wet nightshirt she wore, and this made her feel lost. It is said that a woman loves a handbag. She went outside to look at the object from the other side, and was glad she had, for there was a tag upon which was written: Jane Saint c/o reprogramming. It is at such moments that all memory comes rushing back, but this did not happen to Jane. She now felt confident in opening the rucksack, and found inside a few personal objects. A comb and mirror, a nail-file, a scent-spray, a safety pin, a flashlight, some tissues, a packet of Gitanes Mais Filtre and a disposable lighter, a small book titled: *Further Astral Projections* and a bottle of Guinness but no opener. She put the cigarettes by the phone because she had given up smoking, and then, in case the finder did not have a light, the lighter. There were no maps and no clothes or food. She wished she could recall where she had owned it, and what a 'reprogramming' was. She needed clues. Never mind, this was a start. With the rucksack on her back she felt more confident and strode up the path briskly to get warm, for it was too breezy to be wearing only a wet shirt.

And then she saw the tower against a Sublime sky. She wrestled with an inner turmoil which she knew to be despair. The sight of the tower did not fill her with joy, it looked hostile. It stood on raised ground like a Folly, with steps cut into the rock spiralling around, and the whole resembled an immense phallus, although she knew that there were days when everything looked like that.

Jane Saint mounted the steps and banged on the great door which opened immediately, knocking her over as it swung outwards. Swearing and cursing about design she arose to face a peasant. It was a female peasant dressed in sacking, with greasy hair and warts, obviously mediaeval Germanic.

'What do you want?' demanded the peasant in a strong Yorkshire accent, thus dealing with the obvious.

5

'Sanctuary, sanctuary,' said Jane, gloriously beautiful as Notre Dame, somehow feeling herself as hunched and gnarled.

'Come on in then, and warm yourself.' She actually said 'wahm thissen' but Jane somehow understood.

There was a great brick oven in the corner with wonderful fires raging beneath and a glow from an ashtrap.

'Take off your things and dry them.' She declined. The shirt was already steaming, clinging to her body like stone drapery.

'It's very kind of you to have me in, I was told that I might stay over and that you could help me on my way.' Jane was not certain about that, she only thought that the telephone operator had told her that. It seemed to be the right thing to say.

'I'm looking for my children, and for a kodebook.' Some memory had returned but not much reason.

'A kodebook? You must be from the other place.'

'I suppose so. I'm on a mission, I think.' How stupid she must seem.

'Your children will probably be in the Valley of Lost Children. We might be able to help, but first you must help us. We are making an Anthroparion, and we need a few drops of the blood of a good woman.'

Jane laughed.

'But I am not that woman. Your recipe will curdle if you use my blood.'

'Well let's try anyway. There's nobody else. The vampires won't give us any and mine won't do for certain. When Anthroparion is made he will be able to help you on your way, they can answer all questions.' Very useful! Jane tried to be patient and wait. After all, it was more than possible that this place was Timeless.

From the opposite corner of the room the other half of 'we' shambled out from a narrow closet, dusty and unattractive; an old, selfish man. There were ingrained foodstains on him and his teeth were terrible.

'Are you the new apprentice?' he asked Jane, goggling at her

6

beauty. Before she could reply 'no' the old woman had answered 'yes'.

'Well come here then, I've a few things to show you.' He had all the air of a flasher in a mac, he was fatherly and furtive and much too pale. As she watched, he mixed salt and soot and sulphur, boiled them up and produced gold.

'Crikey!' said Jane Saint, understandably. He took it over to the closet, and flushed it down the oubliette.

'We don't make it for it's own sake you know, just for practice.' He grabbed her hand and while she was worrying about what he was going to do with it, he pricked her finger and squeezed out some drops of blood onto a filter paper. He threw that into a glowing crucible and then added some unholy mix and put the lot into a bottle which he sealed.

'Now we cook him.' And into the great oven went the bottle and then the old woman came near and began to undress herself.

'Time for bed,' said the old man, also undressing. Jane was embarrassed.

'You can sleep over there, under the bench while we make this baby. Don't mind us.' Jane went and crept under the bench with her back to the couple and her ears stopped against the lengthy sound of copulation. She realised as she fell asleep that there was much else she ought to know, or should remember.

Melanie, Dolores and Sybil clung to one another in the Valley of Lost Children, chilled by the wails of others, by the grey mists and by the hard white rocks.

'I think I hear Mother saying she will come to us soon,' said Sybil, only half convinced. The others did not reply. They might be merely lost, or lost forever. There were girls who had been waiting for a million years, waiting for Mother, or for Life to Begin. They needed a clue as to how to escape, so they used the only power left to them, which was wishing. They wished very hard and nothing happened. Then they tried hoping, for Melanie thought of that distinction and it seemed important. As they hoped, they had the idea of digging down into the pebbles, which they did, finding a ring which they pulled, which opened a door

7

into the rock revealing a cave. They entered the cave and the door banged shut behind them. Inside, it was as bright as day and delightfully warm. The results of hope sometimes look very much like astonishing good luck, thought Sybil with incipient irony.

They were afraid, but determined. They walked on around a corner and came into a chamber containing the most enormous woman they had ever seen, reclining like a stranded whale. She was so comfortable and smiling they felt all their problems and miseries fade away. The woman's hands were held in a caressing pose, and they were large enough for a baby to sit in the palm of each. Her limbs were immersed in rolls of solid flesh, her skin taut over nourished fat. Her eyes were hypnotically kind.

'Come to Mother,' she said softly, and they went forward. Her hair was like fibrous rootlets of trees toppled after a gale, earth clinging to it with a fresh smell. There was a creaking noise of something expanding.

The huge finger beckoned. Dolores began to cry, incoherently certain that they must not proceed. She tugged her sisters hard, trying to turn away.

'We want *our* Mother,' she managed at last, and the other two suddenly seemed as if they had woken up. They had a sense of terror, and without thinking they fled away down the tunnel.

'Keep on hoping, don't forget,' said Sybil.

'*Nil desperandum*,' said Melanie.

'*Excelsior*,' said Dolores. And indeed, the tunnel was leading upwards.

Jane Saint was watching the presumably alchemical process, seated by the great fired oven. She was remembering her other life in swatches like fabric samples, coloured and indecisive. Why was she searching for her three lost children – she could not recall losing them, she could not recall having them. It was something ingrained, like instinct, perhaps it *was* instinct. She wondered how old she was, felt certain that it was not less than fifty. Therefore the children were surely not so very little? A late motherhood? Illegal. She got up and went to look at herself in

8

the window against the evening, and knew that she looked young and beautiful by any standards. Had she ever had a husband? Why had they tried to drown her? She must be a criminal. What was the Kodebook?

'Look, something is manifesting!' screeched the old woman. She had flung back the oven doors, and inside, the retort glowed. Jane surmised that it should have melted, so hot was the fire. They carefully pulled out the tripod holding the retort, man-oeuvring with iron rakes until the thing stood on the hearth. Inside, there was a slow cloud of bloody smoke, and claws and scales appeared in it, denoting something not human. As Jane watched, she recalled a dream in which much of this had occurred. Was the other life a dream or was this? It seemed for a moment or so that she was falling between two stools.

This thing in the retort was complete, and the old man came over from his bookshelves to look. He was skinny and bent with an eye that rolled upwards from time to time when he scowled, and stringy hair that he never cut or brushed. Jane loathed him.

'Ask it the passwords!' he roared. He always either roared or mumbled, a sign of a deceitful nature, Jane believed.

'Kodebook Seven,' said the old woman, and the hairs on Jane's arms stood up with interest.

'There's no such thing,' spoke a little voice in the retort. 'Kodebooks belong to people without hearts and brains. The Koran, the Bible for example out of many, tomes by Marx, Confucius and such are all without value in that they only seem to offer the key to a good way of life. There shall be no more Kodes.'

'Sounds like Blasphemy,' said the old man, grinning.

'Sounds like good sense to me,' said the old woman, thinking of how there had been no Good Books which took account of women as other than secondary and of how all Christian females had been judged evil Eve and sinful Salome. A book biased to half the world must be about half rubbish – or rather more. But she did not speak, and neither did Jane, for both knew that it is better to keep the trap shut in certain circumstances.

The old man took the stopper out of the retort and bid

Anthroparion come out. He took no notice when the old woman pointed out that this was not Anthroparion, but a demonic presence. It didn't seem to matter. Jane realised with a strange pleasure that this creature was a blood relative of hers, in a way. It had leathery wings, a scaly tail with a horny point, little sharp teeth in a monkeyish head, and gilded feathers or scales which shone in the firelight. It appeared to be wearing pink nail varnish. It spoke to Jane.

'I have seen your daughters. They have been tested and found strong enough to be women. They are looking for you.'

'I haven't the faintest idea what you are talking about,' said Jane, shivering.

'It doesn't matter, I was just trying to calm your fears. I had the feeling that you were on an important quest, but perhaps you aren't. Important missions are out of style anyway.' Jane realised that she had been expecting miracles. Now, she could not even recall the political problem she had been dedicated to – if it was political. This was like being sent back to square one, she would have to relearn everything to win.

'I'm hungry,' announced the thing. 'My name is Zilp, it's meaningless. Once, I had an exotic Hebrew name but they've given all that up as racialist.' Nobody got that. The old woman went to drag out a sack of flour to prepare some scones. She beckoned to Jane to get on with it but Jane declined, saying that she needed some fresh air. Something was changing. At one time she would have made not only scones but cakes and a batch of bread and currant biscuits and scotch pancakes. Now they would damn well make themselves.

Going down the steps of the tower, she wrestled with Guilt. After all, a woman's place is in the Tower.

At the bottom of the steps was a desert – no wonder so many turned back. It was a temptation. But, ahead also were temptations, coming towards her now in the form of a man. Zilp was watching from the window.

The male figure approached and Jane saw that it wore a doublet and hose in dark velvet with sleeves slashed over gold. It had long fair hair and regarded itself inwardly, which was to be seen from the noble and absent-minded expression on its face. She felt that she could throw herself into the river for the love of such a one. Thank heavens this was a desert!

It seemed for a moment that the figure led a white horse, but she was fascinated to observe that the whole scene changed. The man was in fact wearing farm-labourer's jeans, was naked to the waist, barefoot, his chest covered in a baroque pattern of dark hair, his features clear as if cut from Siena marble. He was hardworking, proud of it. She could bear him ten children as well as keep the house perfect and sit up all night with ailing calves, breaking off to take him ale in the field and to cook huge repasts. But before she could offer her services he changed again.

Zilp came out of the tower and hopped over to Jane who ignored him. He pulled at her shirt, whining not to take notice of them for they were merely the work of a sorcerer, only shifted shapes.

The man now had on a hairy tweed suit and wore a thin pale beard, smoked a knobbly pipe and had untidy hair, leather patches on his elbows and stout stitched shoes on his feet. His eyes were distant with academic problems and male thoughts, kind and strong and yet vulnerable, absent-minded and clever and remote, yet like an uncle, all at once. He smelled of nicotine, which made Jane recall her discarded Gitanes, and of peat and book-bindings. Her heart beat faster and she shut her eyes in bliss. When she opened them again there was a very young man in tight jeans and tee-shirt, lean and innocent, with a little bit of acne marring his immature visage. She glanced at Zilp who clutched his head in despair. Why would he mind her giving herself to one of these? She could not see any harm.

'Test them out by shifting shape yourself,' advised Zilp. 'I can help you to change your shape to some other kind of woman, and you will then see in reality.' Jane shrugged and said why not, for she did not believe him. Jane Saint knew love at first sight when she saw it, and she could have all or any of them.

The man before her now was taller and obviously very strong and powerful, all dressed in black, which set off his close-cropped pale hair to perfection, and his broad shoulders carried a long leather overcoat which was open to reveal a black silk shirt, black trousers and jackboots polished by somebody else. He had a gun and a dagger and an iron cross. Jane could hardly resist running to him and kneeling at his feet, she itched to undo her shirt buttons. But her shape was changing.

She was a little shorter, a little fatter, her face was a little less firm, her breasts a little smaller and a little less perky. Her hair was shorter and full of grey, and her eyes were less bright and her ankles a little thicker. The man blinked and stared at her and passed his hand over his eyes, clicking his heels, bowed and turned to go. The youth appeared and stared at her with empty eyes, the farmer assessing her for work capacity. Then the first man rather roughly suggested that she get herself to a nunnery.

'Do you believe me now?' asked Zilp smugly, preening his gilded plumage. Of course she believed him, for in a way she had always known it had been like this, but had not wanted to know. There had been nothing else to live for.

'Come back into the tower, Jane. Tea's ready.' Zilp took her hand in his sympathetic claw, and sadly she ascended the steps with him.

'But I shall have no friends, nobody will love me any more,' she said, beginning to cry.

'Yes you will, people will love you. Those weren't friends, they were only vampires.'

Scones were handed round, and a massive pot of tea, and Jane tried to cheer up. Her shape was back to normal again but looking in mirrors was not now so reassuring. The question was: what to do now? She had failed to find her lost girls, if she had ever had any, she had failed to find the Kodebook, if there was such a thing and it was worth having, and she had failed to get herself a handsome prince, if they were what they seemed to be. Failed. Failed on all counts.

The old man must have been reading her thoughts.

'You'll be all right girly, if you keep your head clear. Things are changing. They are changing here just like there, but it takes centuries for things to *really* change. It's that kind of world.' Centuries! But she only had a few days! Must get her skates on somehow. He handed her another scone, he didn't seem as sinister now, he appeared sincere. Perhaps he was changing too.

'Go back and accept the situation. Start to do a bit of something real instead of barraging up the old order. You probably thought you were some kind of revolutionary, but I bet you were in the service of those who would cheat you of your birthright.' In her present mood, Jane would bet that too. She felt utterly duped.

'Well I can't go back. I'm dead aren't I?'

'No, no. Dead is dead – how could you be here or anywhere if you were dead? Your body is left behind, this is your real self in the other world, isn't that right Zilp?'

'Right. You can go back, it will be like waking up.'

'Not drowned?' Surely she had felt the water.

'Not drowned. You are confused.' How true.

'But I don't know the way and I shan't know what to say, I haven't done anything yet.'

'Well, if you set off then you will get somewhere, and if it gets you back I shouldn't say anything about all this if I were you.' That seemed like good advice. Zilp brushed the crumbs off his monkeyish jaws and offered to go with her partway, if the alchemists could spare him.

'Easily, I'm sorry to say you aren't quite what we had hoped for,' he was told. Because it was impossible to tell when a 'return' was going to take place except in the case of a few experts, Zilp suggested they simply go for a walk and see what turned up. So after all the leave-taking and thanking had been done they went again into the desert, but this time Jane could see an oasis on the horizon.

Zilp told her how to change her shape if she needed to make tests again. It was easy. Zilp said the technique was called 'plastics' by some.

'It is just as well you are not with your children if you are always like this, you would fill them up with a right load of romantic nonsense, would you not?' Jane had to agree and laughed aloud, pretty certain that she was not always 'like this'. He kissed her hand, and took off in flight, flapping slowly against the lemon-coloured sky.

Jane Saint walked on towards the oasis, wrestling with the problem of hoping, while not knowing what was to be hoped for.

A burning sense of mission was a great help in keeping a person going; she felt pain at the idea of relinquishing it, but knew what vanity it was to think that she could ever have saved the world. Could she have been so foolish as to set out to do just that?

Understanding a great deal less than she had ever understood before, but with great futures stirring within her, Jane Saint just kept walking, and hoped.

It was then that she fell over a cliff for the oasis had been a mirage. She clutched at some small thing floating as she fell and thought: how often does security turn out to be nothing more than a camel shimmering over an abyss?

2. Jane Meets Some Monsters

Falling off an immensely high cliff can rarely be called pleasant, and it was not one of those occasions for Jane Saint. She hated most intensely the sensation of arcing over and over and screamed for it to stop, as if the action was caused by some outside agent other than gravity. She was beginning to feel faint when she came to a bouncing rest in some tangled undergrowth which prevented her from being dashed to pieces. Cradled in inertia she noticed details; in her hand she had a single golden feather. Jane, the practical, peered at it for hallmarks and found it to be 22cts. Hecky thump! She struggled to get the feather tucked away in the pocket of her rucksack for even when dazed she hung on to good sense. She took a moment to be thankful to be alive, but ceased that indulgence when she realised she was being gassed. The odour was so strong and so animal that she expected a herd of hairy somethings to thunder along any moment.

Carefully descending to something like terra firma, she kept her eyes open and her nose and mouth shut as far as possible. It was a pity she had no gas-mask but who could have guessed she might need one? One moment going across the desert and the next falling through space into brambles in what was definitely something like a swamp. She should look where she was going, but she had been holding her head up.

The ground was slippery and, she saw with disgust, swarming with small blobby creatures which continually consumed the grease and excreted it: they wriggled with whipping tails, and were probably the cause of the foul stench. They were like micro-organisms. Were they huge examples, or had she got smaller? There was no way of telling if this was an Alice situation or a demonstration of the loathsome truism that truth is relative. Not that it is, she reflected, it is just that human beings are ill-equipped for judging the relationship of one thing to another, so need a handy catch-phrase for dealing with imponderables. Jane therefore reserved her judgement of the situation and slithered along on the grease avoiding treading on the blobs although the masochistic wretches insisted on trying to get under her feet. As she progressed in the mire she thought once more of what the hell she was supposed to be doing. She had an intense sense of mission but it was impossible to keep in her head for more than a couple of minutes what her aims were. She did not usually work by instinct or intuition, she would have to hope that what she was working for was deep enough in her to guide her, and that her memory would return. She must be suffering from some trauma, but at least she wasn't panicking so it could not have been too bad. She hoped to meet Zilp again, Jane felt that he was an ally.

There must be something useful she could do with a sense of mission and a strong body! Quests. People searched for truth or Grails and such. A search for truth seemed extremely vague – about what for example? Not that she was likely to be waylaid by that truth-is-relative shit, but if a sense of right and wrong is innate then all wrongdoing is purposeful. She was getting bogged down, she went down a slippery slope, drawn along to what might well be a cul-de-sac. She came to a place where the floor was purple and red, like anemones. There were now two paths to take but there was no feeling of a moral choice. She walked right up a small hill between them to avoid being ensnared in a blinkered point of view, and then was alarmed to find the ground rising up beneath her; it formed itself like a volcano with a pool of clear yellow liquid, steaming menacingly. She got around that awful place, rapidly slithering down an escarpment into a deep valley which appeared to end in a tunnel. It was not an inviting tunnel. Thinking swiftly she decided to go ahead, for what was the alternative?

Immanence and death, she felt sure of that at least. Her life must have taught her that, or perhaps she had read it in an essay by Simone de Beauvoir. Immanence. That, being the opposite of transcendence must be detested. Stasis also was useless. On then.

There was nothing to hold onto in the tunnel, and it soon became dark. She fished and fumbled in her rucksack for the flashlight but could not find it so had to backtrack.

'Damnation! Sod it! And other expletives! I hate back-tracking!' cried Jane with sudden loss of temper.

Just as she had found her flashlight, something huge and hairy landed in front of her, splashing up the slime as it landed. It was not benign. All Jane Saint's instincts stood up on their back legs and screamed at her to run, but if she ran into the tunnel the thing would follow. She must frighten it away, or kill it. It was an awful monster. It opened its jaws and she was pretty sure it meant to eat her if it could. It was like an insect illustrated in encyclopaedias, the pages of which fastidious children dare not touch. She could almost see the labels: thorax, abdomen, chitin, mandibles. Her childhood fear of insects returned even though she had progressed to the point of enjoying having small spiders run over her hands. Rationality was not helpful. She shouted 'shoo' at it but it leaned creakily towards her, jaws or mandibles lolling open, eyes focused everywhere.

It jumped up vertically almost disappearing out of sight and returned to the same spot. It leered meaningfully. Jane rummaged through her rucksack for something more effective than 'shoo'. The nail-file was useless, throwing the Guinness bottle would do nothing. Other pockets perhaps. The stench of it made her ill, it had halitosis something shocking.

She found then her O de Lancôme spray, just as it spoke aloud to her in English. (She could have sworn it said with a voice like a wound-down gramophone 'I shall have your blood, the blood of heroines is particularly good'.) This made her act, spraying and spraying the thing with the scent, right into its face. It shrieked and jumped and landed behind her. She sprang to face it, spraying madly, and hope leapt as it visibly wobbled. It toppled over, obviously laughing. The alcohol in the spray had made it intoxicated. She ran for the tunnel, getting mixed up with the scent spray and the flashlight at first, got herself sorted out but sweat poured off her now. Fear was her spur. One was always trying to attain or run away from something and it was not always clear which was which.

The wet walls of the tunnel reflected many little winking lights making her feel watched. Another interesting distinction – being watched and being watched over.

There were no more creatures but she began to feel uncomfortable because of a growing heat and the itching of her skin. Her shirt tore easily, there must be corrosives in the air. She wished there was something to which one could pray for deliverance.

'Oh is there no end to this suffering?' she called, getting an immediate answer by being precipitated down a ridge and landing before a door like a fish's eye. She pounded but there was no sound, it was glutinous, but then its edges drew back and she was sucked in and flung headlong into soft warmth. Exhaustion overcame her and she would have liked to sleep, but curiosity was stronger.

She was in a great domed hall hung with scarlet and crimson, cushioned and soft and full of dozens of little children. She was

17

surrounded. She examined them without speaking, feeling repugnance. They were petulant and quarrelsome, those which were awake nipped and pushed.

Was this where she might find her children? Certainly not the Kodebook.

'Is this the Valley of Lost Children?' she asked.

'Nah, dopey. This is the Womb of The Great Earth Mother and we are the objects of her ultimate motherly love. Welcome. You can stay here for ever if you like.' Jane recoiled from this possibility. 'We shall stay for ever, it's lovely and cosy. You begin to look young again and you can play games all day.' Jane Saint could think of few things less enticing than playing games with these horrors. She cared for no game but chess and had particularly dreaded Monopoly with spiteful brats. A group were at it now, probably cheating. She was here by mistake, she must get out. But the door was sealed. She was filled with fury.

'*Zut! Merde Alors!* May the grandfather of whoever sealed this door be suddenly struck with retrospective impotence and Barber's Rash!' she yelled. The children tittered and nudged. She made an effort to calm herself.

'How did you all arrive here?' she asked one fat boy.

'I have no idea. We here don't think or remember all those intellectual games. We don't live in the past or the future so why bother with it?' This bit of sophistry left Jane temporarily paralysed with its blinding imperviousness. Most helpful. He laughed as she glanced once more in dismay at the door.

'You can't get out you know. Nobody wants to, of course, this place is the answer to everything.' He began to suck his thumb and his eyes turned up in their sockets. Looking around Jane surmised that most of the population was male. The fat boy crouched down and then rolled sideways into a foetal position.

'How old are you?' asked Jane.

'Fifty-two.' Jane sensed something familiar. She knew this kind; they had tremendous power in the world. They disguised themselves with well-cut jackets and rust-free cars. They had solved the secret of life with a wallet full of credit cards. They ran after younger and younger women the older they became. She had long ago decided not to be part of all that nor would her daughters. She might not know what her mission was, but she need not subscribe to somebody else's especially if it smelled bad.

If this was what was meant by not playing intellectual games then a game of ludo might not be a bad idea, even.

Was there a way for her to solve the secret of life? It was an appealing idea. Jane Saint had a nasty feeling that for her nothing would ever be that simple.

There must be a way to break through that door.

The rucksack. A comb, a mirror – but already that was enough. She took the little mirror and comb and began to scrape at the walls of the room as if she was spring cleaning and had decided to redecorate. The glutinous red stuff came away freely and as the walls began to give up the blood of their own accord she was swamped in it. Jane Saint began to worry that she might drown before the contractions got really under way, although the wall heaved in then out as she scraped. The walls then closed in immersing her in scarlet, squeezing her upon a tide, drowning children everywhere, many still asleep not knowing the difference between life and death.

They were all heaved about mightily, worse than a shipwreck, and she swam for the door – surely it must open? There was a female blocking her way.

'What have you done you stupid bitch! Everyone in here was very happy until you came along with your freedom!'

'Did I mention "freedom"?' asked Jane, knowing that she might have done. 'And if I had I wouldn't have said it was going to be comfortable. If I'd been aiming to comfort the world I'd have become a saleswoman in the electric blanket department of Lewis's or Macy's!'

'Well what are you aiming at, opening doors of Paradise and risking our lives on a river of blood? I suppose you are one of those goddam interfering do-gooders, the sort that encourages the lower classes by giving them free education and fancy ideas . . .' The speaker slipped and went under flailing in a pool of foetid rhetoric.

'Don't be silly, you won't die, wake up and swim. You are on the side of Death and Immanence, this is a place of horror!'

'Woman's place is in the womb!' she thought she heard through bubbles. The female surfaced, full of words.

'Women are intuitive and emotional and suited to caring and nurturing and men must be looked after and their egos boosted, the hand that rocks, they are all little boys really it is our duty . . .'

'Oh don't be so bloody stupid,' said Jane giving the creature a crack across the jaw. 'The worst traitors have always been within.' The door was opening slowly. Jane told them all: 'Mothers and Fathers is only a game too, a charade, a denial of human life, slow murder, repression . . .'

'You ain't makin' any sense lady, things 'as bin this way since the Lord decreed and good folks know how to live because it has always been so. Lady hear this, your sort is going against Nature and you'll have to pay the price.' Nature? If Nature were a person would she give a damn about an individual woman? Not bloody likely. To live real lives we must go against Nature for she feeds upon our suffering and death. Jane Saint would have liked to have made a speech out of these thoughts but was there time to deal with hecklers at this stage in proceedings? There was not.

'Swim, swim I tell you and know that it will be worth it!' Many tried to swim against the tide for the first time and had chosen the wrong tide and drowned. Many were lost arguing with one another over finer points, newly fired with the delight of discussion, already trying to vote in a chairman and a secretary, forming a committee deep in the new drug not noticing death all around. There were minutes that would never be read out at the next meeting, over coffee and Marie biscuits.

Jane swam strongly and saw the light at the end of the tunnel and it seemed far away. She was hampered by her rucksack but battled on; it got caught in the undergrowth then, right by the corpse of the monster she had sprayed. It floated on its back, legs folded clutching a small framed painting. Jane got a look at this and saw a portrait of a man looking bemused and frightened. It was titled 'Ghost of William Blake'.

She got herself free of the entanglement and was then washed out into real daylight, onto a beach and over white sand to the sea, reaching cold salt water with intense gratitude and a fleeting sense of unreality. She washed and washed and was gratified to see many others doing the same, the smile of joyous discovery on their lips. They looked less childish out here. But liberty does not suit all for some were washed out to sea and lost.

The sun came out and was wonderfully hot. Her shreds of clothing had all gone and she was tempted to go for a swim and sunbathe. She gave in to temptation and was glad, for the cold and the hot restored her. Always at the back of her mind was the thought that she must go soon.

The beach stretched out on both sides and she could see no other place to go. People were walking away already. Perhaps the cliff behind her had steps?

Yes it had, and she climbed, finding it hard going and hating every moment for she was the kind of person to lose her nerve at heights. It was too much to hope that she would land safely twice. A sense of strangeness overcame her, was this the real world or not? She had once been told that she was living in a world of her own. People said that to make you devalue your own experiences.

She got to the top and dragged herself to a safe distance from the edge but then wriggled back to look at the beach and the sea. There on the beach was an immense woman making shuddering moans, her feet in the sea and a river of blood pouring out of her. Everything returned to the ocean which washed the beach with waves until all the frightful debris was taken by the undertow.

The sun began to set. Nearer the water it descended until its rays were concentrated in a sanguine funnel of fire, making a Sublime spectacle. Jane should have been moved but was on guard and cynical so leaned out and spat instead. Down Sun, down below the water! And down it went like a drowning dog, all the fire and colour and nothing much more in the end, fizzling into the glory down and gone.

'Well, I did something today, didn't I? Although there are many would say my efforts were abortive. But the hell with them: many who claim a respect for life have only respect for dogma and no feeling for life at all. As for tomorrow I must try for something else more positive.'

The moon was up, cool and still, but not yet in command of the sky. Naked as born, carrying her rucksack, Jane Saint trudged off across the plateau, the last reflected light of old Master Sun touching her backside with a decorative tinge of gold and plum.

She looked where she was putting her feet; she could afford no more abysses that day.

3. The Bitch

As she walked along it was impossible not to notice the excellent quality of the grass beneath her feet. It had no weeds, was fine, and had recently been cut. The scent was delicious. This cultivated green, smooth and perfect, stretched with gentle undulations as far as her eyes could see. It was the sort of verdant plain which has grass-widowed millions. Jane thought of cow-grazing, crops, rabbits, but was obliged to dismiss it all as unworthy and to completely ignore a wish for herbicide.

A sound made her look to her left. There was a fellow playing golf with himself and singing 'White Christmas'.

'Fore!' he yelled melodiously and she waved back, answering: 'Not a bad score I suppose?'

As she walked along it was impossible not to notice the excellent quality of the grass beneath her feet. It had no weeds, was fine, and had recently been cut. The scent was delicious. This cultivated green, smooth and perfect, stretched with gentle

22

undulations as far as her eyes could see. It was the sort of verdant plain which has grass-widowed millions. Jane thought of cow-grazing, crops, rabbits, but was obliged to dismiss it all as unworthy and to completely ignore a wish for herbicide.

A sound made her look to her left. There was a fellow playing golf with himself and singing 'White Christmas'.

'Fore!' he yelled melodiously and she waved back, answering: 'Not a bad score I suppose?'

'Don't you know you aren't supposed to be on the green?' called the golfer in altered tones.

'This is common ground, right of way,' called back Jane Saint, taking a chance.

'Be that as it may, I am only thinking of your own good. You might get hit with a ball.'

'What vanity!' she laughed having observed how often he missed, and turned her back hoping that he did not see the situation as a challenge. She heard sounds of protestation, indications that she was considered preposterous; the idiot must only just have noticed she was stark naked – and on a golf course. It was never a bad thing to be considered preposterous by certain types; it might indicate that one was doing okay.

Suddenly and with great force she was projected into another state of consciousness. The golfball had hit her head and knocked her out stone cold.

A little dog came snuffling over the grass and found Jane Saint, victim of a hit and run driver.

'Who's this?' it thought, licking her face although it knew better hygiene being unusually intelligent and well-educated.

'Who is this young woman, here in the middle of the golf course, out cold for six? I could do with a kind mistress, maybe this girl will do for the job.'

Jane began to come round and the first thing she saw was a close-up grin of a red-haired dog. She thought at first it must be an Irish setter crossed with a collie and a spaniel but it gradually became clear that it was a long-haired dachshund; it had very sympathetic eyes and she therefore deduced that it was a bitch.

'Hello doggie,' said Jane, aware of a headache.

'Hello yourself,' replied the dog.

'I am not astonished at anything these days although I still try to preserve my sense of wonder,' Jane muttered in an attempt at sophistication as a means to prevent swooning. 'What is your name?' she asked the entirely pettable little creature.

'Merleau-Ponty,' it replied seriously. 'And yours?'

'Jane Saint. That is an unusual name for a dog.'

'Not for an ex-philosopher's dog, but let's not go into my life story so far. Any name will do for any person or any thing. Any unsuitability is entirely in the mind.' Of course, she should have realised that.

'And are you lost?'

'Not exactly, more strayed. Are you lost?'

'In a manner of speaking, but my quest is returning to me.'

'That's the trouble with quests. Actually I left my owner, the arguments were too fierce. Eventually you just can't live with someone who is widely divergent in opinion to yourself, it becomes destructive and competitive, especially if you suspect them of sophistry. Argument should be creative.'

'I agree, but that's human nature.'

'Canine nature in my case, clichés are never exact.'

'Sorry. My head hurts.' She sat up. Ouch.

'My master was given to some rather horrible ideas which at first look seemed excellent. He quite often said for example that truth was relative.'

'Oh that old chestnut. I hate that. People who go around saying that truth is relative have something to hide, I declare.' Her head was feeling better already.

'Definitely. Only the dishonest spirit could possibly be interested in such trashy transparencies. Philosophical flummery to be sure. The kind of thing a common adulterer will come up with to his wife. It ranks with "it depends upon what you mean by love" as a reply to a plea for love.'

'I know exactly what you mean. I once had a friend made permanently ill by her husband because he could not tell the truth, which was that he did not love her. She could have got over that. It was the flim-flam prevarication that ruined her nerve. Local ideas about truth change but truth is truth anywhere, whether we know it or not.' The dog grinned approvingly, they were already friends.

'Who was your master?' she asked. Merleau-Ponty shuddered and began to tremble about the hindquarters.

'I don't want to mention his name even. He was horrible although such a bleak spirit I felt sorry for him. He never gave me enough to eat and when I complained he tried to reason me out of my hunger pangs. He was one of those unfortunate people who cannot understand that others have needs, and even if they do, believe it is up to them to fulfil them. He was not a sharer. He would not give anything without there being an ulterior motive – and he could see this and it disgusted him. It prevented him from ever doing good.'

'Well to be fair, don't you think that an ulterior motive is there with all good acts?'

'Yes, but that doesn't matter so much as long as the good gets done. Purity of motive is a rare thing, in humans and in dogs.' Jane agreed.

'Your name suggests that you are a phenomenologist.'

'Come to that, your name suggests that you are the mate of an apeish type in the jungle, a dumb blonde with enormous titties, or rather better than you probably are.'

'Point taken.' The next question was, were they going to hang about all day? Jane realised that it was about mid-day, she had met the golfer in the evening. But here, time, unlike truth, appeared to be relative. Merleau-Ponty suggested that they travel together. She also asked where Jane was going.

'Well I don't know, but there is this quest business. It is beginning to be clear to me, but in some awful way I'm having to relearn everything, and yet I have a sense of urgency. It's a hell of a way to make progress. But I must say I'm having an interesting time.'

'Where are you from?'

'Some other level, as they say here. I was to have been punished by brainwashing but I managed to escape for the time being. If I don't succeed in doing something effective while I'm here, I'm pretty certain that both me and the quest have had it – doomed.'

'Dear me, that does sound rather dire.'

'Mm. I have the feeling that I came here in order to change there, but that seems totally illogical now.'

'They aren't very big on logic here, it doesn't have the same standing everywhere, apparently. It's only a method after all. I've heard of your kind of traveller before. They're pretty rare and it seems to have its dangers, it is supposed to be nefast.'

'Nefast?'

'Yes, but it isn't really, just difficult and quite often useless. Not always though. I've heard it said it is the religious maniacs who come off worst, and the drug takers. They go off their heads. But the writers and painters quite often do well out of it, and the occasional sorcerer.'

'And what about journeys the other way?'

'Only when called and then not always. It doesn't do any good, the motives are wrong. Sometimes a few fiends will whizz through for a quick bit of chaos at a seance, just for fun, but there's enough chaos there already, so I'm told, the fun has gone out of it.'

'You mean that the spirits of the dead reside here?'

'Oh don't talk such tripe. You and your individual salvation! Haven't you ever read Jung?' Yes she had but didn't care for him much.

'He had two symbolic systems, one for men and one for women.'

'Well so much the worse for him then. What I'm driving at is his observations about the Collective Unconscious. He didn't invent the sodding place, he just guessed at it.' Oh.

'He noticed that certain people and types turn up everywhere at all times. Here, we are great travellers and very good at light disguise. You can forget about Jung and what he thought about women, you've found something for yourself. Where did you intend to go?'

'Here, I guess. But I can't recall naming it.'

'A world is a world is a world.'

'What do you call this part then?'

'Tarot country this. I thought you must have intended to come to this part, they think they are prophets.'

'I think not. What would I do with the Tarot – tell the future? I want to change the future not peer at the inevitable. I believe that events are constantly working upon one another, everything is in a state of flux and very haphazard, which is not to say that there is no such thing as effect and cause.' She heard the pompous note creep into her voice, a little touch of sententiousness. It was difficult to keep it out when you were telling people what you believed, it so easily became pontification.

'The Tarot is for telling you possibilities, not certainties, so I am told.' Dogs pontificated too, she had caught that tone. They sat quietly a while and Merleau-Ponty rested her head on Jane's thigh. Jane scratched gently behind her friend's ears. She asked the little dog what she was doing here, as a resident.

'Oh, I turn up all over the place in different guises. I've hung around Harlequin, been punched in Punchinello and been an aficionado of the Fool. I have also had a good laugh when the cow jumped over the moon, that kind of thing.'

'I don't think I know what you are talking about,' said Jane, almost certain that really she did. Merleau-Ponty did not trouble to explain, but asked Jane what she had accomplished so far on her mission or quest.

'Well I accidentally got into the Womb of the Great Earth Mother, and aborted her.'

'Oh you! Oh, you're brilliant. I say, that's jolly good that is. Priceless!' The little dog laughed, she fell about, and Jane had to laugh too.

'Oh I like that, you'll get on well here, you must be quite effective.' Such a jolly dog. Jane could not recall when she had found such a congenial friend although Zilp too had proved a friend in need.

'And you seriously meant to change the world and you seriously have done that already! I wouldn't have thought it possible.'

'Well, all that stuff about changing yourself before you are fit

27

to work on the world – it takes whole lifetimes. People might be fit and wise at their own funerals, it seemed to me.'

'You really are a pragmatist then?'

'You mean there's some other way to be?' asked Jane with an ironic toss of her head.

'Not really. Myself, I like a nice fire, good food, plenty of bones, diggable earth, a place to run, affection, intelligent conversation, not necessarily in that order. You know, the things everyone likes. It doesn't have to be action the whole time; if philosophy and action run out of steam, it's a great thing if there's something good for supper.'

'And decent clothes, in my case.' It seemed foolish to want more than a few necessities but there was also an element of brainwashing in too much gratitude for small mercies. She recalled a conversation.

'I think I can find you some clothes if you just wait here,' said Merleau-Ponty, running off. Jane recalled her Grandma recounting what had been said to her when she complained that most women never got a chance to do what they wanted in life, what they were fitted for. A man had said that most women were only fitted for certain things anyway and Gran had said 'baloney'. The man had told her she had no right to be discontent because half the world did not get any food never mind a congenial job. Gran had told him he had missed the point, and if everything he had ever wanted to do had been met with 'shut up and eat your dinner and be grateful' then he would be hopping mad too. It was all very sad. But what next? How to go on?

The idea of male dominance was an archetype, one of those 'relative' truths, not an Absolute. Jung must have known this but chose to interpret the facts to suit his own purposes. Maybe if she met the right archetypes she could do something about overthrowing the oligarchy.

Merleau-Ponty returned, dragging some clothes in her mouth. She had brought a sleeveless Fair-Isle pullover and a pair of Y-front underpants which mercifully smelled unworn. She had found these in the changing-room at the clubhouse. With the aid

28

of the safety-pin from her rucksack Jane got dressed in these garments. Merleau-Ponty said she looked very original. The clothes were adequate, the weather was not exactly cold. Jane confided her recent thoughts to her friend.

'Worth a try. The Wise Old Man for example.'

'Where might he be?'

'Depends. As this is Tarot country, he might have turned up there. Let's mooch along and see what turns up.'

'Crikey, I'm remembering things. I'm looking for my three children, and for the Kodebook that isn't supposed to be any good.'

'Well, one thing at a time. If I smell anything I'll let you know. I wouldn't worry about your children, pups have tremendous survival potential. I've had two litters and lost the lot, children have a right to their own lives.'

'But they are supposed to be helping with the Quest.'

'They'll turn up. And as for a Kodebook, I can't think that with instincts like yours you would need it.'

Jane felt heartened and flattered. They set off. Just to go looking around and see what turned up? Why not?

What the hell else was there to do on a perfect fairway? Play golf?

4. Swings and Roundabouts

They were walking over the great flat plain, a green prairie, brilliant, emerald, poison, verdigris, grass of grass, flat, smooth, the fourth note in the colour scale: green. Large, huge, ending at the edge, it is four-sided, and over these four edges there is nothing. This is a flat world, poised over a frightful drop into Infinity with invisible trails where Things fell off; Jane and

Merleau-Ponty had been trudging over this for a long time and Jane's hope of anything turning up had worn quite thin. They were both extremely glad to see something in the distance.

'I don't smell anything living yet, it is probably a small building,' said Merleau-Ponty, who was tireless. Jane was tired, but knew that this must be metaphorical. An experience of tiredness felt much the same anywhere and in any mode – her feet dragged. She made an extra effort and they pushed on a little faster, and it became apparent that the thing in the distance was moving like some kind of machine. There was no breeze so it was not a windmill. There were other things too and as Jane strained to see far ahead she tripped and fell her length over a tree root.

'Oh shit! I've barked my shins!' she wailed. 'Whoever would have expected that in the middle of all this?' Merleau-Ponty laughed at Jane struggling to get up and hopping about, ha ha, barked her shins, ha ha!

'Oh shut up you dumb beast, I mean it, look at that.' There was a contusion on each shin. Merleau-Ponty looked ashamed and sat holding up a paw for forgiveness.

'Honestly, there I was walking along, and in all this space there has to be one tree root and I fall over it. It has made me feel quite sick.'

'If tree roots are causing you *Nausea* then we might get some intelligent light on something before the day is out,' barked the little dog, cheering up again as Jane stroked her head. Jane said she was suffering.

'Give up your suffering,' she was advised, and came as near to kicking a dog as she ever would. There were sounds in the distance which it soon became evident was a mixture of music from a steam organ, and a fairground barker, or shill. They heard the end of 'My old Man says Follow the Band' followed by 'Way Down upon the Swannee River' mixed in with an energetic 'roll up roll up' routine. The shill ignored them, he was talking to himself. It looked like a fairground in full swing but there were no customers except themselves, and Jane felt sorry for the man who must surely feel silly? He was a small man, fine-boned and good looking, with an American accent and a Mickey-Mouse tee-shirt.

'All the secrets of the Universe are here, you can tell anything from watching and listening to the shows and truly wonderful characters we have here.' Merleau-Ponty sniffed dubiously. 'You can tell all the secrets of the Universe from one ashtray, so I've read – if you've got the time,' she said. Jane laughed because she had read that herself in Ouspensky, but as she had given up smoking the information hardly pertained.

'Come and see the Emperor, the Empress, the Magician, the Hierophant, the High Priestess, the Lady Justice, the Lady Force, the Great Judge, the Fool and the Lovers who never leave each other.'

'I suppose these are the lovers in the valley,' Jane murmured to herself about something else she had once read. She could not recall her last lover and didn't want to. Must be getting old. The shill was still rabbiting on, it was a great routine, he had the air of one who could sell anything to anybody. But they had no money and at a fairground you don't get very far without that.

'. . . a mystery figure with no flesh to his bones, and one of the great inventors of all time, Lady Temperance who created entropy and the oldest hermit ever, he never goes out. And a man who spends his whole life hanging by one foot from a tree. Ride on the Wheel, whirl in the Chariot, see the heavenly bodies in the firmament, and meet the One who is All, with a million faces!'

'That sounds hard to take, two faces is bad enough.' The little dog shrugged, she didn't expect perfect integrity in anything.

Well, so it was a sort of Blackpool or Coney Island. They walked past the shill who kept on with his routine regardless, stepping around melting candy-floss. Underfoot was now dust and gravel, quite awful after the cool grass. A lot of the sideshows seemed to be closed, with the tarpaulins laced up, and the Chariot, a kind of Big Dipper, was temporarily out of service. As they passed the coconut shies, Jane could have sworn she saw a row of human heads on stakes, but Merleau-Ponty drew her attention ahead to a show which was open. When Jane glanced back she saw only coconuts.

And there ahead on a small draped stage, was a gloriously beautiful woman dressed in a robe of gold Lurex, slit to the thigh, decorated with a variety of clanking ornaments, her hair done in hennaed plaits and frizz. As they watched, she took a hypodermic out of her sleeve and gave herself a swift shot in the thigh which unfortunately was less than perfect because of numerous scars.

'This must be the High Priestess,' said Merleau-Ponty. So this was a repository of illumination, truth, wisdom? At a sideshow? Still, things are not always what they seem, so Jane introduced herself, and said that she would like to ask some questions if possible. Her apology about lack of funds was loftily ignored.

'I don't speak to people directly, I have dialogues.'

'I see. With whom?' asked Merleau-Ponty impatiently.

'With the Hierophant mainly. We work together.'

'Somebody call?' came a bored voice from behind the dark red drapes. After some fumbling, the Hierophant emerged triumphant. He was quite impressive. He stepped forward arranging his robes which draped very well being made of nylon jersey. He had a vermilion cape with a turquoise border over a blue robe which showed a white undergarment and white shoes, which on closer inspection turned out to be tennis shoes with crackle-finish Blanco. The most amazing part of his costume was his hat which to Jane resembled nothing so much as a phallus – but, of course, this might be one of those days when everything – but that hat really did, it seemed even to have a pink satin foreskin.

'Hi,' he said. Jane thought that she ought to be feeling more respect, she was being attacked by feelings of falling short somewhere.

'I would like to ask a question,' she said as respectfully as possible, determined not to be taken in by appearances. She must clutch at straws if there was nothing else, anything might be helpful.

'Fire away.'

'Dear Hierophant, can you tell me how I may improve the

position of women in society?' That had a lot of it in a nutshell, surely.

'You may pose the question,' he said, fumbling with his robes which could have used a laundering. He finally got himself seated in a canvas chair, and the High Priestess reminded him that the question had been posed. He stroked his beard which was wearing thin from this action.

'Well it all depends very much upon what is meant by "position" and "society", not to mention "change", do you agree my dear?' Merleau-Ponty felt that she could have interpolated a few choice comments. The High Priestess said she agreed but it was not convincing.

'In our Cosmos there is a great and wonderful history of order and meaning, but that is history.' Perhaps that sort of contradiction happened a lot in a timeless zone.

'Now all is chaos,' he said with relish, not unlike a Welsh bard declaiming. 'Minor beings are out of place, they ride in the Chariot and swing on the Wheel, they climb the Tower and float down unharmed, they run amok, they sleep without sequence and pattern, when and with whom they like.' Jane thought it sounded great.

'Everything in the Universe is changed every time you breathe or drop a pin, with or without angels.'

'Yes Hierophant,' said the Priestess not displaying weariness. Her eyes had a distant look.

'But long ago the Judge spoke and said that Order should come out of Chaos and that there is no other choice. Lady Justice agrees with this. It is logical that chaos rules, okay?'

'How can there be any logic if Chaos rules?'

'Chaos is where you get Order from, aren't you listening woman?' he said testily. Merleau-Ponty could not resist joining in, and asked if Lady Force could not do anything about this situation. The Hierophant frowned and indicated the NO DOGS ALLOWED notice pinned to the front of the stage; it was an old notice, well piddled upon.

Suddenly the back curtains parted again, and a woman of a certain age appeared, her hair hidden under an elegantly wrapped turban, her body clothed in a yellow silk shirt and a narrow black skirt. Jane gasped with disbelief. Merleau-Ponty was not surprised.

'I told you so. Wherever signs of Sartre are, you will find Simone.' What signs of Sartre, Jane requested.

'The tree root, of course.' Would Sartre come too? Very doubtful, there couldn't be anything much here to interest him.

'Well good grief!' was all Jane could manage.

'Better not pursue the Goodness of Grief any more than the Isness of Is at this stage,' said the High Priestess, trying to get the limelight back off the new stage centre. 'Good morning Simone, I hope you have brought some of that stuff you choose to call Reason?'

'I merely happened to be here, I was not prepared. It was sheer contingency that made it happen. When you are still seeking things, contingency is an amazing force to be reckoned with.' She spoke in French, but a dwarf was wheeling in a small video which displayed the whole scene with English sub-titles.

'Ms de Beauvoir, may I say how much I have admired and been inspired by your books, especially *The Second Sex*.' Jane's speech flashed on in French, she hoped it was a good translation.

'Thank you. Very happy to have contributed. What is this old sod doing sitting here farting away, doesn't he know there is such a thing as real wisdom?'

'Women have no notion of real wisdom, they never understand it when they hear it,' he said spitefully and indeed unwisely. Blood pressures went up, adrenalin flowed, but Jane and Simone exchanged glances. Simone smiled ironically and quoted extensively from her book, the bit about women's work. '. . . this labour does not even tend towards the creation of anything durable.'

'But it is changing is it not?' asked Jane, trying to recall why that must be a silly question.

'Things improved, then got worse. There are difficult stains in the male mind. They made us what we are and then blame us for it, and dislike it if we try to change.' It sounded somewhat hopeless.

'No win!' came the timely shout of the shill, causing Merleau-Ponty to laugh. Jane pulled herself together.

'We came to consult the Wise Old Man, I want to improve my position in relation to reality.'

'That cannot be altered,' chorused Simone and the little dog.

'I mean . . .' The dog chided Jane, telling her how powerful words were, that linguistics was not just junk, it was important to say exactly what you meant. The High Priestess butted in, swaying about sensuously as she spoke.

'The Hermit says that words distract, when he is meditating he concentrates on just a few syllables, he says it is very restful.'

'What utter nonsense,' said Jane contemptuously, 'what utter dogshit.'

'Hey watch your language!'

'Sorry. Look, there was a dialogue, do please continue.' Might as well try to gain something from all this.

'What was the question?' asked the Hierophant, and they all knew that he knew, really. Jane longed for a really Wise Old Man, to climb on his knee and ask questions about the Universe. Daddy, is there such a thing as equality of the sexes? What would he have said? 'The question is irrelevant, we are all brothers.' Except for the sisters. Simone de Beauvoir laughed to herself and made some notes in a little book.

'*Tant pis* for the Tarot,' said Jane to her friend. 'I thought it might be special.' The High Priestess overheard.

'People nowadays use computers to get information, but the Tarot still knows more that the questioner, you didn't frame your question properly.'

'Bollocks,' said Jane suddenly out of patience.

'Is this a *contretemps*?' asked the Hierophant. On the video that got translated as 'against time'. Jane realised that the first question should have been whether the Old Man was Wise or not, and she should have asked it of herself. Some people have to keep learning the same lessons she reflected bitterly, she could have kicked herself except her shins were already hurting. And having Simone de Beauvoir here and not being able to talk properly, it was galling.

35

And then there was the leathery flapping of wings overhead, and with a sulphurous swirl of cosmic halitosis Zilp landed beside her, grinning. Ms de Beauvoir stared at Zilp in utter disbelief and the sub-titles stated: 'My God, my liver must be in an awful state!'

'Jane, for fuck's sake, this geezer isn't a Wise Old Man, you'll be a dead duck if you take any notice of this stuff they hand out here.' The face of the Hierophant darkened but the High Priestess giggled. Merleau-Ponty was growling, her hackles up, and this purely animal reaction to a creature of darkness amused Jane who did some 'there there' pats, not meaning to be patronising.

'You are both my friends, and I want you to like each other,' she said. Merleau-Ponty came as near to biting a hand as she ever would but Zilp grinned agreeably.

'I was just coming to similar conclusions myself,' Jane told Zilp. 'You're a kind of guardian angel to me, you must have sensed I'd taken a wrong turning?'

'To be truthful it was sheer contingency brought me here,' Zilp explained causing Simone to do a double-take.

'Still, what would I do without you?' Jane asked Zilp not expecting a reply.

'Get conned by stuffy old farts like thousands before you I expect. You really must try to wake up a bit, you are not attracting helpful influences sufficiently. The next thing I hear you'll take yourself off to some Egyptian doctor and get yourself circumcised.' Now the Hierophant was really mad, his face looked as if it had been left out in the rain for a week. His hat was wilting.

'This is all most disrespectful, wisdom is no longer understood, some ancient truths have been in existence for six thousand years or more.'

'Then it is time they were changed,' said Zilp and Merleau-Ponty muttered something about relative truths going stale in the breadbin.

'Come on Jane, let's go in search of something more interesting. Get on my back.' Jane found this idea most exciting and climbed aboard and then reached out for Merleau-Ponty who was yapping with glee but Zilp took off too quickly leaving the little dog jumping up and down in frustration. The High Priestess was dancing round the Hierophant singing a little song.

He's a guru, he's a guru,
He's the kind of guru who ought to be in a zoo.

Simone de Beauvoir turned and walked away with her hand to her forehead, and then she stopped to make some notes.

'Oh Zilp, we've left my dog behind,' wailed Jane in acute distress. She looked at the fairground and saw the High Priestess doing a striptease.

'I can't stop now, she'll turn up later,' Zilp said over his shoulder. 'That place is dangerous; didn't you notice the coconut shies?' Jane clung on fearfully as they gained height hoping that the danger mentioned did not include canine intelligence. Soon, they were over the edge of the square world which now looked quite small, no bigger than a card-table.

'Zilp we seem to be absolutely nowhere.'

'Best jumping-off point for somewhere,' he said airily, flapping smoother and faster. Out here there was nothing to relate to, how was it possible to navigate under such circumstances? Her transport must have powers she knew nothing about. They were thousands of feet from everywhere and she felt very tired indeed. The Tarot had proved to be very wearing, and she had only met a bit of it – as she began to doze she seemed to remember a time when she had consulted the Tarot often and the I Ching and all manner of Oracles. That must have been time at the ashes of hope when it seems that nothing less than a revelation will save the day. How pathetic. Somehow, she must find direction that was more positive. She dreamed she heard a voice say:

'Adjust her drip nurse and check that temperature. Respiration correct?'

She had her arms around Zilp's neck, but her grip slackened with every sleep-layer through which she descended.

5. Heroes or Villains?

Jane Saint was aware of a distant buzzing, a whirring much as if someone were cutting down old trees with a ripsaw. Sometimes her afternoons had been ruined by such sounds, as she was sunbathing or trying to get the babies to sleep, or reading an improving book, a saw would rip away at the suburban silence. She tried to turn over but had that paralysed feeling which sometimes assails the Half Awake.

Her mind dreamed of children, three little girls: Melanie, Dolores, Sybil. The dark, the tawny and the fair. They were playing in the garden, they were playing at Cat's Cradle, that game which is sometimes invested with tremendous significance. The three of them wove complex patterns and then unwound them into a single loop, an eternal thread. There had been idyllic times, or there would have been without the ripsaws. Power noises shred the nerves, and in this case drowned the wing-beats of Zilp who laboured to save his heroine. He was reaching behind him with his arms to try to hold her secure, but this was becoming a terrible strain. His muscles ached frightfully and she felt very heavy.

The noise in the air was one which Zilp had never heard before; in the place of his origins there was no machinery. Mills were not generally recognised as being Satanic and the Gates of Brass had been forged by hand.

Jane woke and only gradually recalled where she was.

'Crikey, how long have we been flying?'

'Ages,' Zilp replied. There had been nowhere to land. When

he lowered altitude he could not be certain that he was not ascending. Without point of reference or interest it was not possible to be balanced or upright.

Something touched Jane's head from above, if there was an above, startling her so much she yelped. Zilp grasped her harder, sinking into what surely must be 'down'.

There was a tremendously loud voice in the air, then, filling them with awe, and a violent wind. Zilp shuddered and muttered: 'Oh no, not Him!' But he need not have worried, his fear was a Pavlovian reaction to Loud Voices.

'Try to get the harness around you and belt it up through your crotch and over your shoulders onto the central shackle-pin,' boomed and grated the voice. Oh miracles, airsea rescue – Jane immediately became all action, she knew what to do, she had seen it on television. There were two of these harnesses, and with difficulty she got herself and Zilp fixed up although his wings were not allowed for in the design and he looked most uncomfortable with them screwed up in lumps. The helicopter rose and fell, the straps went tight or got in a muddle but she managed somehow, driven by necessity.

'What happens now?' asked Zilp anxiously, looking up at the flying machine with suspicion.

'Up we go, you can have a rest,' she told him smiling, so he hung on with his claws and hoped for the best – it was no time to tell her that his instincts were full of dire warnings.

Eventually Jane lay in a heap on the floor of the helicopter which had proved to be as difficult to get into as a boat at sea, watching anxiously as one of the men on board helped Zilp. Watching Jane with a great pleased grin was a large white Alsatian dog which as soon as it saw Zilp began a menacing growl. The fur on its neck stood up and its teeth were bared.

'There, there, nice doggie,' said Jane feebly, stroking this beast of doubtful intent. It clearly did not like demonic presences, few dogs do until they become familiar.

'Zilp is nice, good doggie,' warbled Jane at a loss, somewhat frightened of the animal; all his ancestors had been trained to guard fiercely, from her closeup view of his jaws she could see he would have no trouble in fulfilling the command 'kill'. But he stayed, there was no command. Zilp's helper stroked Jane's hair and she looked up to see a vaguely familiar face virtually drooling with sentimental recognition. It had a greying beard and moustache the texture of steel wool, unkempt hair in strands obviously meant to cover a high forehead and a shirt neither conventional nor Bohemian open at its neck. There was a coarseness in the skin texture indicating careless washing and heavy drinking, and the watery eyes in this face had a pathetic and yet sly possessive expression.

'I am your husband darling, you will recognise me when the shock of this terrible adventure wears off. My darling, I shall look after you now, there is nothing more to fear.' She stared into the eyes of the stranger quite bewildered and repelled. Husband? Surely not? There was a strange scream: Zilp had fallen out of the helicopter as it banked, the scream diminished and the dog barked and barked. Jane could do nothing and the man claiming to be her husband looked not displeased. She wept and called the dog stupid for being so delighted which it obviously was.

'That's my best friend you dumb hound!' The dog said nothing, it was the taciturn type. Could Zilp possibly make a safe landing with his remaining shreds of energy? How profoundly she hoped – could it be possible that the world really was unjust and that Zilp had lived only to sacrifice himself so that Jane Saint could live? No! It must not be! Better contingency than such an awful plan.

The man shut the door which immediately made Jane feel a great deal more secure and then he helped her to unfasten her harness. She suspected that he must have purposely tampered with Zilp's harness. His hand caressed the back of her neck, stroking away tension, causing more. She looked up at the man through tears and he seemed quite handsome. He offered her his handkerchief to dry her tears, and when he was thus brought into focus he had lost that attraction. The only way to look at some men was upwards, through tears, if you required illusion that was.

'Darling, I do love you, truly I do,' she heard her own voice say, tremolo, like a bad tape-recording.

'It all depends upon what you mean by love,' said the white dog but his face was impassive, nobody heard but herself. She looked at it just grinning the way dogs will; a handsome beast with a perfect head and a good coat and clean teeth and tongue.

'There, there, boy,' she said and it just looked soft at her except that she could have sworn it winked. She telepathed friendliness and the idea that he had been hasty in wishing Zilp to leave the helicopter and a message returned immediately to the effect that anyone with wings should not take up space in a mechanical flying vehicle. So. A telepathic dog. Of German extraction like Merleau-Ponty, but how different they were.

'For a start Alsace is very French and I am a guard-dog and she is only a pet,' said this remarkable dog. 'And my name is Volto.'

'Pleased to meet you, I am Jane Saint.'

'You must think I'm very dumb, you are already well known, one of the few to get through here and make friends. I do hope you aren't going to upset things too much, my master doesn't like things upsetting.' His master – her 'husband'?

'No, the pilot. He doesn't say much especially to people like you.' Like her?

'Well one has only to look at you to see that amongst your many mongrel ancestors there must have been a Jew or so.'

It was a distinct advantage being able to communicate in silence, forewarned was forearmed.

'What do you symbolise I wonder?' she asked without thinking.

'Symbols are never aware of their own import. I didn't even know I was a symbol. I'm probably not. I'm just a dog who likes doggie things.'

'Maybe you can help me. I'm here on a mission but I keep suffering from amnesia.'

'Maybe you're on a quest to get your memory back?' Jane had never realised how witty dogs were until recently, it was a fact not generally made enough of in dog books.

'Vee har runnhink hout hof gass,' said the pilot. Oh God our help in ages past don't let us down now, came out in a tense mutter from the other man. Then he seemed to change his mood and said 'Well we must just hope to find that great petrol station in the sky' with a British grin, all grit and bad fillings.

'Well if you are my husband what is your name?' she asked under the impact of a sudden burst of intelligence.

'Hugh Kolz,' said he. Wrong name, meant nothing. It was the sort of silly name that hard-up novelists get off an ouija board.

'Zer mist hiss clearink,' said the pilot whose face she could not see. He wore a leather helmet and goggles. They all looked to confirm this statement – they were not even at a great altitude. There was a discernible building, a long road across a sunlit landscape.

'I hem loosink heltitude,' said the pilot between clenched teeth as if it were usually beyond him to land safely in a normal fashion. Volto caught Jane thinking this and giggled.

'Dear little wife,' murmured Hugh Kolz, stroking her hair which action she detested. Some people do not know how to stroke hair for the pleasure of its owner. It was strange to experience something compelling and repulsive at the same time; she longed to relinquish responsibility, be given gentle orders, smiled upon indulgently, approved of for merely being alive and doted on for trying to be very very good. And she wanted to sock him in the teeth and kick him in the groin and eject him from the helicopter because he was a total threat to her existence. He had to be an impostor, she could never have married this.

She ignored him, watching the ground below, marvelling at the fortuitousness of a gas station at the very time when gas was needed. It was that kind of happening that made simple people believe in an Almighty and His personal intervention in human problems. These days, Jane might just buy a bit of synchronicity but none of the Divine Intervention shit.

The pilot got them down with much circling, as near to the gas pumps as was safe, and had the air of one who has done something extremely clever. When they were all outside they found the weather scorching hot, not surprisingly as this was clearly a desert complete with cacti. It reminded Jane of a Mexican movie set; there was a rundown building upon which was written 'Cantina' and the sand was piled artistically. There was a rock behind which she fully expected someone to be sitting under a huge hat – there was in fact a guitar being strummed. In the distance were purple sierras. The cantina had swing doors – maybe Gregory Peck would come ambling out with a dimple in his chin? The road on which they stood was deserted except for a small figure running. It did not stop, it did not see them but ran on by, looking very much like a rabbit. Jane thought it said 'I'm late!' in a choking American screech.

'Stay Volto,' ordered the pilot unnecessarily as Volto was telling Jane that there went Brer Rabbit again. Hugh said he must be seeing things, he could have sworn he just saw Bugs Bunny.

A shambling nondescript man came out of the booth by the gas pumps, apparently not at all surprised to find a helicopter wanting refuelling, grumbling that the pipes weren't long enough, could the thing be moved a bit nearer without them thar blades goin' around? It could, apparently, and the pilot went off to see to this important detail.

But what about money, had anybody got any? The husband went through his pockets but could find neither loose change, credit cards nor cheque-book. Must have left them in his other jacket. They must all need some refreshments as well as the gas; Jane rummaged through all the small pockets of her rucksack. The Guinness bottle was non-returnable but she found a few coins. Even if they had no money the gas was now going into the tank she noticed and they could hardly get it out again. The man came back for payment.

'Anybody know the exchange rate for five hundred lira, ten dirhams and two French francs?' she asked hopefully, reserving the golden feather because she felt convinced it was priceless. This wasn't bad, finding odd bits of cash, not for mere synchronicity that was – but the man didn't think much of it.

'Ain't that just like a dame?' he grumbled, going back into his booth to continue his intellectual appreciation of the SF story in his copy of *Tits and Bums*. Jane had thought it a good coincidence – what the hell, there would have been no Thomas Hardy novels at all without coincidence but it would not pay for the gas as it was, so they all trooped into the cantina to see what they could do.

There was a worn-out looking woman behind the counter, lolling forward to display a handsome but neglected cleavage, and without moving any more than necessary she turned the money over and then threw a handful of tokens at Jane.

Well, in that cantina there was a fruit machine and Jane decided to try a bit of gambling to see if she could make a profit. The pilot walked around pretending he was not there, swinging his helmet and goggles in his hand and whistling a bit of Wagner which sounded very like 'Hello Dolly'. Hugh looked dignified and Volto came over to Jane as she manipulated the knobs with intense concentration. She had a distinct memory of being quite good at this game, and already she was coming up with goodies. Only her fruit and the rattle of winnings could be heard except for the drone of a large fly. It did not take her long to win a pile of tokens that would have made the person who had rigged the machine to lose far more than it won for its players to have apoplexy, but this was because the dog Volto had been influencing it in their favour. He was not only a telepath but a very intelligent telekinecist.

Jane got her tokens changed into cash and she gave some to the pilot to pay for the gas, and then asked for the menu. Eventually they all got themselves seated and then Jane went to do the ordering, to the displeasure of Hugh who clearly thought that was his job. The woman behind the bar told Jane that never had she seen such luck, it called for a celebration, and opened a large bottle of red wine for them to drink while the food arrived. They were to have tortillas with chilli and beans and steak with chocolada, a speciality of the house. Jane could see over the bar into the kitchen where there were three women working. They looked ill and haggard and utterly woe-begone, not unlike an early Bratby painting of his once wife, Jean. These women clanked as they moved about preparing food because they were chained to the kitchen sink.

'Isn't that illegal?' asked Jane, pointing.

'It's their own choice like mine,' the barmaid told her, showing a much finer gold chain round her ankle which was fastened to the bar. 'Nobody has to do that work in that way.'

'What is the alternative?'

'Starvation.' Well of course there was always a choice. The three kitchen hands' chains were around their ankles and wrists but were long enough for each to get to any part of the kitchen. They had to be careful not to get themselves muddled up so when they had wound their chains together they slowly unwound them again, like a slow dance. The steaks were smelling good.

Hugh Kolz came over whispering about not talking to inferiors but Jane ignored him until he actually tried to pull her away whereupon she asked permission to go into the kitchen and talk to the women. Permission granted.

'Do you actually like working here?' Jane enquired.

'Oh yes, it is very good here. We eat every day and we have each other for company. Once I was alone all day.'

'Where was that?'

'In a small house on a housing estate, I didn't have a proper conversation with anyone for seven years.'

Jane felt like crying, it was unthinkable.

The steaks were done, served with the bitter chocolate sauce which was surprisingly good. Jane had to fetch the dishes. She observed that the women were not Mexicans, but all cats are said by some to be grey in the dark.

'Why are you here?' asked one of them, handing over the tortillas.

'I am on a mission, a quest.'

'You are seeking something? What is that?'

'I don't know exactly, I shall know when I find it.' The women including the barmaid found that highly amusing, they obviously thought Jane must be crazy. Fancy looking for something when you didn't know what it was. They always knew what they wanted – but of course it was no use looking for it.

'Which of those men is yours?' asked the third woman.

'None of them,' she replied including Volto.

'You have no man?' this was shocking, she had no security, how would she live?

'On my wits and nerves. Earn, like you.' And yet not like them, please, for they told her all their money went to the boss who was not here.

'Wouldn't you like to escape?'

'Where would we go? There is nowhere else.'

'But the whole world is out there if you only seek,' she cried, knowing damn well she was being glib.

'No. Not for us.' They were like battery chickens which can no longer fly. Freedom meant nothing desirable.

'For Christ's sake where's the rest of the bloody food?' Hugh Kolz suddenly called out in irritation. Little smiles were hidden from him but Jane glared at him.

'Tell me your names,' she asked the three women.

'Melanie, Dolores, Sybil.' Well, that kept her quiet all through the meal and nobody else had any conversation.

It was a very subdued party that finally got into the helicopter and took off again. Jane waved although there was nobody looking up. She saw the place was called 'The Cantina of the Three Graces'. Very Romantic.

'We cheated on the money,' she said unhappily. She turned the change over and as she did so it turned to dust.

'It was Fool's gold,' said Volto.

'Everyone is dishonest at times,' said Hugh Kolz piously, so it might not have been the chilli and chocolada making Jane feel nauseated. She thought of her golden feather – that was real. She hoped against hope that Zilp had landed okay and that she would see him again some day. It was not every day that you made a good friend.

'I'll try to be friendly but that creature gets my back up,' sent Volto. Jane patted him, good boy. Where were they going, were there any plans?

'Hit hiss a secret teer laty,' said the pilot, looking as if he had played at pilots as a boy and got stuck with it. Jane found him

ridiculous as well as sinister. But just so long as she could find
people like him ridiculous maybe she herself was not in totally
bad shape? She should be grateful he had rescued her, she hadn't
said anything to him but he was so unapproachable. Anyway, the
whole set-up didn't feel quite right, she could trust neither of
these men.

If she could get her head sorted out a bit more, things would
begin to shape up. In spite of everything, Jane Saint felt
optimism. Volto had gone to sleep with his head in her lap.

His animal warmth was a great comfort.

6. Meetings and Partings:
Jane Sorts Things Out

Jane Saint had dropped off to sleep leaning against cuddly Volto,
lulled by the persistent noise of the helicopter. The pilot
remained taciturn and she had stopped listening to the man who
claimed to be her husband. He could be no such thing although
the journey through to this place was certainly bad for the
memory. The possibility of not recognising her three daughters
haunted her; she felt certain that she was a mother because as
she woke she found herself gently stroking scars on her belly, her
hand slipped in through the Y-fronts. When she opened her eyes
she saw Hugh Kolz watching her lustfully so she stopped and sat
crouched with her hands around her knees, looking out at the
scenery. There were distant mountains but they were flying over
many lakes and islands with a river running through like a vast
estuary. The place looked hot and treeless. Volto began to whine

as she thought of trees. There was something moving on one of the islands.

Jane realised how bored she had been; the least sign of life made her excited.

'Pilot, I suggest we investigate,' pompously said Hugh, also interested in this sign of life. He couldn't seem to say anything without trying to make it sound like an important instruction. The pilot nodded curtly, nobody consulted Jane or Volto. They circled in to the island.

'I sometimes have *déja vu* experiences,' murmured Jane unthinkingly, aware too late that this might be an unwise revelation. She needed her secrets. Hugh looked very interested and asked her what they were. She felt violated when he looked into her eyes so looked away and had it taken for charm. She could still feel his hypnotic power willing her to speak.

'I suddenly felt that I knew why I was here and that I could accomplish my mission. I felt I would be reunited with my daughters and that they would help me. I felt it had happened before.'

'Suppose you found that your true destiny was to find your children and kill them, like Medea?' This repulsive idea made Jane put her arms round Volto and hide her face. The dog telepathed: He is an evil old bullshitter only trying to scare you, with that type it passes for flirting.

She recovered her composure and gave Hugh Kolz a withering glance which he countered with one of open innocence so clear and pure it had to be fake. Only good liars look so unflustered when challenged thought Jane Saint the Sensible.

When they were low enough they could see figures on the island, and then Hugh saw some kind of boat also with figures, approaching the island. What gladdened Jane's heart most of all was the sight of Zilp flying around the island. As they got closer she saw that he was chasing off vultures, one of which flew up and gave them a nasty jolt by batting against the blades of the helicopter.

Dear Zilp, he must have landed and made a recovery, thank goodness for that. She had hardly dared to think about him but had kept faith that he was not dead. Volto told her that he for one was not glad to see Zilp but she sent back a request to try to be friendly. Volto said okay, no fighting, he was sorry about the last scuffle, he would behave for Jane's sake. Jane was pleased that she was getting on so well with animals these days, it seemed like a good sign. It was said that animals preferred good people, and if this was so then perhaps she had good in her; she had hardly known who or what she was for some time. She resolved to make greater efforts to get her brain clear. It was all very well being on a Quest but it was downright stupid that she did not really know what it was.

'Well if you'd only asked me,' sent Volto. 'You came here to try to reform the minds of men from within to speak with the archetypes face to face. I can read your mind where you don't seem able to read your own.' She looked at him with open mouth and eyes – of course, exactly so! But why didn't you tell me before?

'I don't listen in to everything, and anyway I could hardly believe you didn't really know your own business.'

Well, yes. She must somehow change things in this place so that the way men and women were could be altered. She had come with the idea that she could change things which had been taken for granted for thousands of years! She began to weep with relief that her mind had been cleared, and at the impossible enormity of the task ahead.

'My dear lady wife, whatever is the matter?'

'I think I must be premenstrual, please don't let it worry you.'

'I won't. Pull yourself together.' What a loathsome human being. How unkind.

'Yes dear, I'll try,' she said in an itsy bitsy voice all pearls and treacle, the kind of approach a dried-up old gas-bag was sure to love. She must now keep her secrets. So this was what Mummy had meant when she called Saint John – or was that St John Stevas – a humourless old fart?

Three figures on an island. There had been an island in an Algernon Blackwood story with some very strange goings on, some ghostly and awful feelings. There had been an island in a

Graham Greene story with an underground world with a golden po but this was neither of these islands, although it did have a tunnel leading to it, and it had strange goings on. It was an island from which the occupants could not escape because they could not swim, and water had filled the tunnel as they emerged. They had tried to swim but almost drowned and they had a horror of water, which was understandable because they had once been immersed in it up to their ears, in the dark, for a long time.

They had come intending to help their Mother with an important mission, to the place where ghosts lurk, where all thought begins, where dreams form, where inspiration is hatched and ideas whispered down the telephones of the human brain. They had gone somehow wrong because of inexperience which is why they had been playing Cat's Cradle on an island. They didn't like the look of the vultures and wished they had some bread to throw but they were not on a picnic and in any case vultures do not care for cold beef sandwiches with or without pickle.

They plaited grass and made parallels, a cross, the double cross, the star, the knot. It was lovely, they had kept themselves amused like this for seven years which seemed like one golden afternoon. They had learned things: the twofold nature of Time, the four elements, the secret meaning of a crucifix and the eightfold path. They contemplated mandalas. They saw a pattern in the knot of the universe, they felt they could weave all things. But when they tried to swim they could not, which is paradox or irony, or a damned nuisance.

Melanie was the first to see the figure on the raft which floated slowly towards them. They could hear hounds baying hungrily.

Who might it be in the boat?

It was the Gatherer and his hounds, and it was not a raft it was a longboat and his five hounds smelled sweet and tender meat. The Gatherer whipped them often to keep them savage, to make them eager to hunt.

The boards of his longboat were brown with blood that had dried in the eternal sun and stank of corruption and his forearms were stained with the juice of his gatherings. Any being who strayed near his river was his natural prey for it was the River of

Lost Aspiration, which was why these three girls had arrived there; they had not been aware enough of how important their part might be, they were too young.

The Gatherer owned the fishing rights but he was not allowed to land for if he did he would be doomed to dissolution; this was a curse put upon him by a sorcerer too terrible to name. He hated all things but he loved to eat what he could gather, his hatred was also love; he was a very confused man.

He was old and naked, withered by the burning sun but wiry and strong with a brilliant glint in his eyes. He saw three beautiful young girls and whooped with joy and the girls clung together in terror. The vultures circled in but one of them certainly was some strange vulture. Zilp batted them out of the sky and one fell into the Gatherer's boat, alarming the filthy mindless hounds. Volto caught this thought of the Gatherer's and retorted that they lacked only education and proper environment. The hounds fell upon the vulture and consumed it rapidly. Blood stained the waters. The girls wailed, staring at the Gatherer, his bony frame and knotted muscle, his long thin penis and scrotum dangling sadly, his dreadful fingernails, his curving toenails. They caught the smell of him and screamed for help. They heard the helicopter and saw Zilp and almost swooned with fright: which was worst – a horrible old man who exposed himself or a thing like a pteradactyl?

The Gatherer leered, spittle dribbling and the three girls were paralysed with fear. The girls looked up and their three heads and braids of hair made a picture of beauty, their hair streamed as the helicopter came near with its occupants marvelling at what they had found. The first out was Volto who rushed up to Zilp who had also landed, meaning to be friendly but Zilp spat sulphuric acid at him, making it necessary for him to go for an unexpected swim. Jane came next and ran to Zilp with open arms, to love him.

'Darling Zilp! Whatever is going on here?' She kissed him on the neck and the watching girls thought this pretty soppy. A golden feather fell from his neck revealing a small patch of human skin. Jane put it with the other and looked around, smiling at the girls. Hugh was disgusted with her kissing this creature, he had not been too pleased at her intimacy with the dog. He did not approve of humans and animals exchanging affection, it was not hygienic. Come to that, kissing humans was suspect.

'Jane for God's sake come away from him – he spits sulphuric acid.'

'So does Bette Davis and I don't believe in God.' She went to the water, right near the Gatherer who was reaching out with a boat hook hoping to catch the skirt of a girl, so Jane grasped it to be helpful, thinking he wanted to land. She had hardly registered his awfulness; she was so overcome with delight at finding Zilp. The Gatherer looked baffled and angry and the hounds howled.

'Get off hussy or I'll have you too.' He would have her anyway, she was a lovely wench. He would eat her alive, warm blood, pulsing heart, he would feed on her pain as old men will feed upon what woman will allow.

'Mummy!' screamed Melanie. 'Mummy, Mummy, look out!'

Everyone stopped. What? Her daughters? These three lovely girls? No woman could have forgotten such children. And yet, why should beauty be better to recall than ugliness, what kind of love would that be? Her emotions were not engaged, there was something wrong. First her husband and then her children and she could hardly feel a thing. Just echoes of love? Was she enchanted?

'Mummy! Mummy!' It was a cry for help and this she responded to – she wrestled with the Gatherer and his hounds, driven to madness, love and the need to protect driving her; the slavering hounds did not have the measure of her for she kicked one into the water with her bare foot even as she almost toppled the old man. She was as strong as he was and it was his greed against her maternal instinct, she would fight to the death. Hugh Kolz did nothing. Volto came out of the water angry at Jane for kicking a dog.

'The ghastly things will eat me if I don't get the better of all in that boat, can't you help instead of moralising?' she answered desperately. Volto, seeing the truth of this picked a fight with a hound but found himself attacked by four which brought out all his considerable but usually controlled aggression. Hugh Kolz, man of contemplation, did nothing. He remained detached. He went over a few of the more obscure points of the Tao to keep in mind the fact that we are civilised beings and not beasts, victims of our baser drives, and to calm himself because he felt nauseated. The Gatherer smelt foul.

'Some husband you're turning out to be, why don't you help?' screamed Jane, hauling a hound off Volto by the scruff of its neck.

'I do not approve of violence.'

'Sod that, what about loyalty?' Hugh went to the three girls to comfort them but they had no confidence in him and turned to one another in a huddle.

The Gatherer got his hands on Jane again trying to drag her into the boat. The noise they were making was a true pandemonium. But Jane hauled the Gatherer to land and threw him down and would have leapt upon him but he instantly began to change. He became infirm of purpose, blurred like a watercolour and went out of existence in a shadow of grease and a whiff of bloody dust. Gone.

The pilot of the helicopter, still in his seat shouted 'hip hip hooray' but nobody took any notice, it lacked conviction. The girls began to cry and giggle as the hounds turned tail and splashed off across the river, paddling as fast as they could. Volto had not only shown them that they were cowardly fighters, he had been giving them a lecture on decent behaviour, cowing them with strong words. Zilp flew at them in a parting flap and hiss to make them swim faster and circled back to land at Jane's feet, whereupon Volto walked off a distance, head up to conceal his nervousness.

Jane hugged her daughters, all was now well.

'Mummy let's go back, it's horrid here, we can't do any special missions after all, let's go back.'

'I don't know how to go back just like that, my darlings. But now we're together again maybe we can find a way. Anyway, you've already helped to get rid of that awful old man, I'm sure that's useful.' They knew they were being consoled with fibs and they wanted to go home and sit on the lawn and have tea and sandwiches and watch the bumblebees go into the flowers. Home.

'Well, darlings, if we go on for a space maybe we shall find someone who will be able to direct us? Then we'll decide what to do. I agree you are far too young to be in a place like this but as I recall, it is the lesser of two evils.' Well then, what was the other evil? They could not remember, but Jane could, and did not want to tell them. Zilp had something to say, he held up one claw mockingly as if in school. The girls looked at him with awe. Was he dangerous?

'This is a very good friend of mine and his name is Zilp. He has been helping me to look for you.' She introduced them and Melanie asked if he liked to be stroked.

'Of course, doesn't everybody?'

'No,' muttered Hugh. The girls stroked Zilp, and then he told Jane his thoughts.

'Seems to me that if you return now with the job half accomplished, you will not like the future. You have to change the setting somehow so it will be a good world for these girls.' Well, Jane had known that but Zilp had put it tactfully. Everyone looked at the girls, three innocent, perfect young females. All hearts were touched at the thought that their futures might be bleak. If they had been ugly, or, as the pilot thought 'dogs' – making Volto wince – then would so much have been made of their fate? No. But beauty has uses, for it now tipped the balance in favour of battling on somehow; Jane thought that between them they could make a world where souls could grow in whatever kind of body – if dualism made any kind of sense. Jane always felt that flesh and spirit were one but recent adventures were making her think twice.

She drew herself up together inwardly but suddenly the whole scene was disturbed once more. The pilot of the helicopter had crept out and then suddenly grabbed the girls and was bundling them into the machine, ignoring their squeals and shouts.

'I say, have a care,' said Hugh thinking he was being a bit

54

rough. Zilp was looking into the distance and saying something to Jane: 'I see an image of three tired and ageing women eternally wandering round a clean house, their many children gone away, the linen cupboards full, the windows shining, love withered away . . .' Jane sprang into action hurling herself towards her daughters but the pilot pulled a gun out of his zipped jacket, protecting himself by pointing it at Dolores' head.

'Stant back! Zeze girls shall be mine! Zey shall become mothers of fine young men!' Dolores ducked and Jane leapt kicking high at his wrist but he fired at her and blood spattered them as she fell backwards, knocking over Hugh Kolz who was actually about to do something. The pilot pushed the screaming girls over the sill and Zilp flew at him but got two bullets which grounded him and he dare not spit acid for fear of touching the girls. He picked up stones and hurled them into the blades which the pilot had now set in motion but it was not enough; the door was closing but the ladder still hung, Jane clinging to it – Volto scrambled over her back snarling but got hauled in too and a jackboot in his jaw. 'Stay!' roared the pilot and Volto cowered, still as he could.

Jane got her hands on the sill but the pilot stamped on them but still she clung on to the ladder as the machine rose into the air. She clung in agony with some mad notion of trying to bite his ankle.

'You bastard, those are my daughters!'

'You vair not too sure of zat! Ve need girls like ziss to train for zer Great Purrpuss!

'Release them, stop this – pig – beast –idiot . . .!'

'Ve shall make zer Master Race!' Jane tried to swing her legs sideways to get into the machine but the immense draught from the blades prevented this piece of circus entertainment and the pilot reached out with his boot and kicked her head and as she fell she knocked Zilp out of the air too for he was trying to fly even with his torn wings.

They fell together into the River of Lost Aspiration.

7. Come The Revolution

Zilp was saved from sinking by his spread wings but Jane sank deep. He floundered around trying to dive and Hugh was just about to dive in when she floated up, hair spread like fire in the sunlight and they pulled her ashore. With much pumping they managed to get her to eject water, and Hugh, forgetting revulsion administered the kiss of life without success; Zilp tried and they were rewarded with her consciousness. They wept and laughed at once. Some time elapsed before she could get up and walk around and take off her clothes to dry but when she did the image was of a bruised butterfly emerging for the first time; she seemed about to fly into the sky to find her lost daughters but she was earthbound. She thought she heard a voice say: 'Well, watch the water level carefully, we don't want to get the sack for negligence.' She did feel unwell, partial drowning is not good for the human system and shock produces strange effects, thought Jane, glad to be alive.

'Is there nothing we can do to get the girls back?' she asked in some despair. 'There must be something.' Zilp looked embarrassed, he was feeling humiliated because winged creatures are no match for helicopters. When he told Jane this she wept again and held him close to console him; Hugh averted his eyes from the sight of a naked woman embracing a beast, or perhaps merely from the sight of a naked woman. Jane loved Zilp, he had become close and necessary, she had not dared to believe that he had fallen to his death, it would have been too great a sorrow.

And it would have set the work back unthinkably. Work? Yes, not forgotten this time. Altering the basic setting of mankind, clearing out all the rubbish of long ages in men, and women too – it was no small task but if the theory was correct then the method should work. What she needed was knowledge. The High Priestess had been no Wise Old Woman and as for the manifestation of Wise Old Man with his silly hat, if that was wisdom or knowledge she had done with them.

Hugh very sensibly pointed out that although Jane's wounds were not deep they needed attention, they must move. They had a choice of trekking off in no particular direction or floating downstream in the longboat, for the punting pole and boat hook had both gone. Zilp tried to fly but his wounds ruined his style. Jane was trying to be brave but the loss of her girls had shaken her and almost being drowned was not good for the resolve. Tears ran down her cheeks but Hugh looked at her with no sympathy. He felt that she should pull herself together and stop snivelling, which, as far as moral judgements go – not far – was right.

There was a great booming voice in the sky which made Hugh jump for only he heard it; the voice rumbled and echoed something about a mote and a beam in his eye.

'Didn't you hear that?' he screeched. No, hear what? He passed his hand over his brow, much as Byron might after a bad consignment of dope, and said he must be hearing things, it was time to be moving. Jane and Zilp exchanged glances, but she put her dry clothes on again. They all voted for getting into the boat although the idea of floating downstream did not delight Jane, but she sat in the prow, her hair spread about her shoulders still drying, blood dried on her and flies buzzing everywhere, attracted by the nauseating odour of the boat. There had been many grim feasts here, there was the stench of living pain as well as corruption. They pushed off on the slow water which did not look fit to drink. Would the sun never set?

The sun never moved, it was eternal High Noon.

Jane became delirious after some unmeasured time although she did not realise it, but she kept slipping in and out of other

57

realities, her grip on place being slackened by her fever. Sometimes she saw herself as if from outside, and this could afford amusement.

She saw herself as if in some old movie, walking into her marital bedroom to find Hugh Kolz engaged in some physical act with a young girl, and his horrified face making her laugh at them both. So that had been Mrs Kolz's unrealised fate; usurped by a concubine. Fate worse than death.

Every time she returned to the longboat it seemed that she felt a little better, but Zilp was holding her hand and looking worried. Could she die here? Was she dead? No, that had been explained. Was there death after death? These were large questions floating in confusion and they disappeared as she found herself shopping in a supermarket, so heavy-hearted, wave after wave of awful pain flooding her heart, radiating out to her extremities, a continual mourning but all there was to see was a *hausfrau* buying margarine and then she was back in the boat and glad to be there. Better to die with friends than to feel loneliness like that.

And then around a table in a room with a familiar feeling. Yes! The KB7 meeting! She was the envoy of these people, contact, at last!

'Oh, what luck finding you,' said Jane but they all turned appalled faces to her and a man with a black beard grabbed her arms from behind. What?

'Who are you?' a severe woman demanded harshly. They did not recognise her. No wonder, because she had made a mistake. The feeling tone was the same as the KB7 meetings but everything else was different. These people were revolutionaries, the walls of the stuffy little parlour were covered in pictures of Lenin, Stalin, Che Guevara, Angela Davis, Martin Luther King, Martin Luther, Sylvia Pankhurst and Mary Wollstonecraft. There were some excellent watercolours of the Tower of London, the Bastille, a castle in Spain, the White House and the Kremlin. Not at all amateurish.

They were certainly revolutionary, which is to say going round in circles. Why were they all dressed in late nineteenth-century costume? Very elegant and uncomfortable, hardly action clothing. One lady toyed with a fan and a man stroked his pistol suggestively. There was a samovar with a pot of raspberry jam nearby and the room was full of smoke; one of the women rolled herself a cigarette from the contents of a pouch without even looking what she was doing. In the centre of the chartreuse chenille tablecloth there was a black globe with a limp fuse. It bore the word 'bombski'. A good time was being had by all.

'I am Jane Saint, I am with you by error.' It sounded better than 'mistake'. They sighed with relief and recognition of her name, they had thought she was a spy and furthermore they had been wanting to meet her. Have some tea, have a little cake, put some jam in your tea, have a cigarette. No thanks, don't smoke.

'We think you can help us, our aims are identical.' Well maybe, but she did not feel to be their kind of political, especially if they thought they were communists which was not clear. The communist religion exploits women as ruthlessly as any other, she reflected.

'We have an assignment for you.'

'Well maybe I can help, that will depend.'

'With this plan you will be able to liberate women for ever.'

'Tell me more.'

'We have a foolproof method of eliminating men.'

'How drastic.' Men must be good for something.

'We have it all worked out.'

'I don't like plans too well worked out, the imagination gets cramped.' There were gasps of indignation.

'Whose side are you on, woman?' bellowed a pretty fair little thing with pink cheeks. It was not really a relevant question, all Jane wanted was to have no fear of flying, to save her own life, to have a life based on praxis, not to be a bad sister and not to live for love alone. Compared to them she was a reactionary.

'There are no sides. The question of freedom for women to live as well as other human beings is a very pressing need to which I have devoted myself.' She could be succinct when she wished – had she ever put it so clearly to herself before? But who was she working with, that she could not recall, perhaps her group were divided as most groups are, into factions more or less radical.

'This meeting is *in camera*! You must swear never to reveal a word to anyone.' They looked very suspicious, like all revolutionaries, suffering from paranoia.

'Paranoia is not a disease, it is a warning system.' They all heard the voice of an invisible presence but Jane knew it came from Zilp, he was holding her hand.

'Don't go yet,' they told her, observing that she was fading around the edges. 'We have an invention you must help us with, it will permanently change the world.' Zilp tugged at her hand.

'You must fit a capsule into the correct place in the Central Thought Library, we have it here.' The man with the gun rose and took down the picture of Lenin behind which was a safe. He took out an object like a crystal ball. Jane thought they must be nutters, and if the invention was real, it was open to abuse. And there was another matter.

'But some of you are male – are you sacrificing yourselves and your sex to this cause?' They looked puzzled, as if the question had no meaning, moustaches twitched, deep voices ummed and aahed. The women looked enigmatic. Poor brainwashed men.

'This capsule will act upon the future but also retrogressively. We shall always have been known as Womankind and reproduction will be by parthogenesis and in exceptional cases, cloning.' Crikey! She next asked them how they came to have such advanced technology and also why they did not complete the task themselves.

'Russian scientists are decades ahead of all others of course, and we are now all too well known, we are watched constantly.' Everyone fell silent, waiting. The jam was passed round for the tea – it was quite nice in tea once you got used to it – and Zilp tugged harder, pleading with her to come back to the boat.

'In the name of Marx what the devil is that!' screamed someone seeing Zilp actually manifest. One particularly boring woman reminded her colleague that in a rational ideology there is no such thing as a devil, but then she saw Zilp and fainted. His wounds dripped onto the Kazahkstan carpet and holes were already sizzling away.

'Jane, take no notice of them they are stupid, come back with me now.'

'But Zilp, don't you think we ought to take advantage of modern technology in matters of importance?'

'Not like this. It's not up to anyone to wipe out half the universe, it can't be right.' Thinking of humiliations suffered by one half of the universe by another, Jane was not so sure. The apparent leader of the revolutionaries was saying that she would give Jane the exact references needed for the placing of the capsule. She thought.

Suddenly she was back in the longboat, telling Hugh:

'I know what you were up to working late at the office.' He went pale.

'B-b-b-b-but,' he stammered satisfactorily looking extremely guilty. Then she was back in the room, taking the capsule and the instructions.

'Jane Saint you are a fool,' said Zilp.

'Of course, only a fool would try to change the world for the better.'

'Good luck, comrade!' she heard the noise of rushing water. They were approaching a cataract and Hugh was shouting to her to wake up. But Jane felt suddenly full of strength and power, no cataract could stop her now. All she had to do was find the Thought Library. She looked up at the sun, high noon. She took a cheroot from the top pocket of her fringed buckskin jacket, bit off the end and spat, asked Zilp for a light and he obligingly breathed fire. She put her booted feet up on the office desk and pulled her stetson down over her eyes.

'Now I can see my way clear,' she told them. Zilp wondered how he could get her out of this phase and into something safer, after all, he was male and stood to lose a lot, it was the principle of the thing really though. The noise of the cataract was immense. But it was siesta time for Jane Saint, Sheriff of the Badlands.

8. Just One of Those Days

There are times in all lives when courage has departed, when moral fibre weakens, when stamina for the fray is at a nadir. Some believe that conjunctions of planets cause such times and if this is true then Jane Saint's planets had got their knickers in a twist. She sat in the longboat with her companions on the River of Lost Aspiration, her quest seeming hopeless, even considering that she had a neat answer to everything in the capsule. Was she sickening for worse fever? She began to fear gangrene, worms, suppuration, disintegration. Zilp had said paranoia was a warning system, and everything felt real. The hygiene of their conditions certainly left much to be desired.

It seemed that there was not, nor had there ever been anything in her life worth living for. She felt that she had not been blessed with true love or affection, with worldly success, or achieved any spiritual growth.

If she had talent it had been ignored, if she had beauty it had been exploited, if she had love it had been stolen, and sex could always have been better. Her mind was a wasteland of facts and her emotions a morass of negative charges; anguish, self-pity and hatred. Was there no way to annihilate this horror?

'Cheer up Jane,' said Zilp, observing her to be on a bit of a downer. 'Cheer up girl, something is sure to turn up soon. We can't go on for ever like this.'

'Can't we?' she droned, convinced that they could. 'We have to find the Thought Library and as it is the largest building ever you'd think we'd be able to see it from here. It isn't visible.

Maybe it is a myth. And by the roaring noise I should think that a cataract is going to swallow us up directly.' It was true about the threat of the cataract but the boat drifted very slowly and they could not work up a decent panic to spur action.

'Maybe we should paddle for the shore?' Zilp suggested. When drifting downstream it is hard to get action going, but they did paddle and got stuck in some weeds. The current was stronger than they thought when they tried to get across it, another few yards and they would have been swept up into the mainstream, where dreadful adventures can have only logical endings and truly fantastic luck never occurs. They squelched ashore, Zilp helping Jane, and what a sorry crew they looked. They tied the longboat to a shrivelled willow which had wept itself to sleep in loneliness, lulled by the mournful music of an Aeolian harp which hung in its branches.

'I think I see our destination.' Zilp pointed with his claw at some distant structure, looming in isolation on the horizon. It must be the Thought Library. It had to be.

'Do you think we'll get there before nightfall?' asked Hugh wearily. In Eternal Noon? Jane looked at him, through him, she could feel nothing but contempt for this person and was ashamed. Why should she expect more of him just because he was male? Answer: because he was so patronising, and when it came to difficulties she expected him to live up to his own estimation of superiority. She reached out to his hand to give him a little strength but he withdrew it roughly. Sad churl!

Jane could not understand people who needed affection and yet refused it, or perhaps did not even need affection? The very concept taxed her imagination. It was impossible to force affection or it became something else. Let him be, poor sod.

The building on the horizon seemed larger and nearer already, and she had not expected to get near so soon. She stopped for a few moments to ascertain something: she had entertained a suspicion that the thing was moving towards her, like Burnham Wood. But it stayed still when she did, perhaps it was very cunning: the Thought Library must be the most intelligent building of all, it contained a record of every thought which has ever occurred, right from the beginnings of thought; it had to be bright with a memory like that. Jane thought it would be very useful to have a membership card then she could draw on the world's thought supply any time – she would be able to find out if the writings of great philosophers were what they really thought.

'There's somebody creeping about over there,' Hugh observed, pointing towards the building, now on the horizon, and not looking very large.

'Seems to be looking for something.' Zilp flew a bit to get a better view but it was a strain. They shouted but there was no response. They came to the figure, an ageing man with spindly limbs and a hang-dog expression.

(N.B: Giving a dog a bad name is a semantic offence which certain persons should know better than to commit. Yours faithfully, Merleau-Ponty.)

'Oh well, hi there,' he said crouching on his heels, looking as if he was trying to hide something with his shabby caftan. Hugh seemed to be too tired to take his position as head of the family so Jane stepped in as spokesperson.

'Hi. We are seeking the Great Thought Library, I suppose that is it over there? We also need to get cleaned up and healed, we've had adventures on my quest.'

'Oh. A quest. Jesus man, isn't everybody on a quest?' Jane thought: no answer to that.

'What are you looking for – gold?' she asked.

'In a kind of way. I've been sent out by the old alchemist guy and his woman to look for the Philosopher's Stone or I don't get any dinner tonight.' He looked tearful. 'My blood sugar gets low if I don't eat and then I get depressed, man – hey, you don't happen to have any food, do you? Vegetarian organic grown food?' Sorry no. What tower? Oh no – not back there again, oh damnation, was he sure?

'Sure, I'm sure. We're on the side of Perpetual day and the other side, believe it, is Perpetual night. You been here before, man?'

'Yes,' said Jane, irritated at being called 'man' although being called 'woman' wouldn't have sounded any more polite.

'Well, come back with me, maybe you could put in a good word for me about the supper.' Jane set off thinking perhaps the Alchemist would know the way. They were all in a bad temper. Even Zilp was hypercritical.

'You can't have been looking very hard, and it isn't very nice of you to think only of your own stomach when you can see what a mess we are in,' he snapped. The man crumpled up blubbering, whining a sorry tale about how he was all mixed up, he'd been on pills, his head was out of focus and cheap brands of Californian wine were slowly poisoning him. Oh dear.

'Oh, look, do stop that, we'll help you look if you like.' In fact within minutes she thought she had found it but it was only a bit of blue bottle glass on which she managed to cut her finger.

'Ouch!' she said, originality failing. Hugh took the glass and examined it.

'Poison bottle, you may have inadvertently injected yourself with something deadly.' He didn't offer to suck the wound and Jane was past caring. Then Hugh thought he had found the Stone, yelping 'Eureka!' But shit, it was only an alabaster egg of the kind that people with artistic pretensions bring back from Florence.

'I know somebody who's got a whole sweet-jar full of those in the bathroom,' Jane said.

'Doesn't everybody?' countered Hugh.

'Well as a matter of fact it does *look* like a Philosopher's Stone, I've seen enough to know there is a distinct resemblance although the real ones are more kind of translucent than that,' Zilp interpolated.

'I thought there was only one!' Hugh said acidly.

'Well, if there's only one I've seen it turn up all over the place, it must travel fast.' So they packed it in and went up the steps of the Tower, Jane leading, and she paused and turned to the man and asked him who he was – she'd need to know his name if she was going to put in a word for him.

'Well I'm known as Hotroach Dobson but here I'm called Merton. I'm the last, but the very last of the Bohemians, Beatniks and Hippies.'

'Pleased to meet you, I'm Jane Saint, that is Hugh Kolz and my friend is Zilp.'

'Jeez. I thought he was an hallucination.'

'I thought you were going to say that,' spat Jane's friend. 'Things do change – in my earlier days you found genuinely interesting people in the Underground.' Jane knocked on the door and remembered to step back this time, almost sending Merton flying. Oops sorry!

'Well look who it is, come on in, I've got a very interesting experiment going on. This time I'm certain we've got Anthroparion.' Just what she needed, it would answer all questions. There was a joyous yapping and Merleau-Ponty rushed between the alchemist's legs almost toppling him, jumping up to Jane in sheer delight. She was all wag and yap, quite incoherent with pleasure. Zilp seemed quite pleased to see her and apologised for taking off too quickly and Jane had the presence of mind to hug them both equally.

'Shut the door do, some people behave as if they'd been brought up in a barn,' said the old woman crossly.

'Some of my best friends were brought up in barns,' Merleau-Ponty informed her, and Hugh laughed indulgently.

'And who is this quaint little soul?' he enquired.

'Merleau-Ponty, my friend, and this, my little dog, is Hugh Kolz.'

'I am her husband.'

'Oh, I didn't know she was married, she doesn't wear a ring.' Jane signalled to let the subject drop but everyone's attention was on the glass retort cooling on the work bench, where something swirled interestingly. Would she be able to enquire about the wisdom of putting the revolutionary capsule into the Thought Library? How would she know if the answer was true?

'We'll bake some bannocks after this,' said the old woman and Jane was just going to offer to make up for not helping out when Hugh replied.

'Certainly madam, it is years since I did so but I daresay I haven't lost my touch.' Surprises! Well good, let him have a go, it was a good sign. Merton was moaning softly at the mention of food, he'd give his soul for a bannock just as long as he didn't have to make them.

Anthroparion popped out of the flask and expanded.

'Greetings!' he said in a very foreign accent. He was a very Romantic figure and Merton was most impressed.

'Man I dig your image, I really dig your image!' The Anthroparion was dressed in animal skins with much bright embroidery, big fur boots, his long hair hung in dozens of plaits and he wore many beads of bone and ivory and had pouches slung about his shoulders, and three bright green feathers bound together on a leather thong. He was very greasy and grimy and had the worst set of teeth Jane had ever encountered.

'Told you so!' said the old woman spitefully to the Alchemist. 'You never get anything right do you?'

'Oh heck, not *another* Shaman!' he groaned. 'We're always getting sorcerers looking for healing remedies and other potions these days, how come?'

'I enter this world by any hole available, I have been out of my body two hours now, it lies in my village in Finland. Happy to be of service in exchange for a certain remedy.'

'That's the trouble with astral travelling, it's so haphazard,' said Jane. Merleau-Ponty sniffed the Shaman and found him okay, he smelled of reindeer and seal and fish, quite nice really. Zilp agreed, it was haphazard, he'd had no intention of getting into any adventures with Jane; it had been pure chance, but he was glad it had turned out this way. The Alchemist said he must try a new recipe, it must be the blood of a good woman that was so rare, and got a smack on the head from his wife who was fed up with him. The Shaman grinned at this, and started fishing in one of his pouches, finding materials for cigarette rolling.

'Hey man, is that dope?' said an animated Merton.

'What is dope?' asked the Shaman and Merton just stared at him unbelieving. The Shaman put his request to the Alchemist and his wife while he was rolling up; the Chief's daughter lay dying in childbirth, they could not stop her bleeding. The whole village was in mourning and it was urgent. Could they help?

'I daresay I could whisk up a little something,' said the old woman, 'but it'll take time. We want some bannocks first.' Jane was outraged – it sounded urgent and she said as much and the woman was beginning to explain when Merton asked again about the dope.

'Well this is my special mixture of pleasure herbs, perhaps you'd like to try some, I'm in no hurry.' Jane was very agitated. Irresponsible weirdos rolling up joints when a woman was dying in childbed, not to mention her own Quest – one look at the old woman told her what happened to females who bent their neck to male ideas of pleasure-seeking and Jane saw something looking up at her from the spectrum: Red! Her depression had been severe, she was full of the stuff that turns to rage at provocation. She pointed at the Shaman, her finger accusing; Merton was beneath contempt but this one should know better.

'You! You would neglect a dying woman for a party, you are typical, *typical* of manhood, you just don't care what happens so long as you get your pleasure.' The freckles on her face stood out like spatterings of gold mud, her hair crackled like an electrified lion's mane and her lower lip stuck out looking ready to catch her staring eyeballs. Righteous anger was firing her, and the Shaman bowed.

'Madam,' he said politely, shambling backwards to the door but Jane was after him. Hugh stood well back, blushing because he had been very interested at the thought of trying a smoke, he had always wanted to have a go.

'Don't you dare try to escape when I'm telling a few home truths, you skunk!' She dashed out a hand at him but missed, sending a glass retort to the floor where it exploded violently into green smoke. Jane's anger took her forward regardlessly leaping with both hands outstretched, just right for being thrown by anyone with elementary knowledge of Judo which the Shaman had not, he was unused to any kind of combat, he was a mystic and so respected at home that nobody had ever tried to attack him. He believed she was a very attractive demon, the kind he often dallied with when off on these trips. Unusually fierce, should be quite good fun. Nobody intervened so Jane got a purchase on him, twisted one hand in his leather thong and thumped his head with her other hand. This completely ruined his continual inner chanting of magic syllables and made him even less aware that another blow was arriving on his nose, or that she tugged his whiskers but he felt her fingernails scratch his cheek. Hygiene in his culture being what it was, the bacteria on his skin immediately set about building new housing estates in his dermal layers; they had the outdoor paintwork finished and the honeysuckle planted and the milk ordered and a window-cleaner booked before the first drop of blood had beaded on his greasy cheek.

They had carpets fitted and the second generation ready for college by the time he felt the pain and were rocking in granny-chairs on the back porch knitting socks for the starving foreign babies before he said 'Ouch!' For the first time in his life the Shaman hit another human being. It hurt his hand, he could not understand what people saw in violence. Jane was blind with fury and saw the world through tears, sweat and green smoke. Hugh stood ineffectually pleading, rubbing his hands together like a fly on sugar. Merton said 'hey cool it, man' but Jane was deaf. She tugged at the leather thong and it snapped and the three green feathers floated away and were drawn into the fire, disappearing in a moment.

The Shaman wailed 'Aiee aiee you shabby bitch, now I cannot return, those were my flying feathers, I can go nowhere without them. It would not have mattered dallying a while, there is Infinite Time here, it would only have been a few hours absence when I returned but women never understand these things. Stupid cow, I am doomed and so is the Chief's daughter.' He fell to wailing but everyone else was very quiet.

Jane was covered in shame. Of course. How could she have been so stupid. Oh crikey, oh double crikey. Wasting energy fighting over principles of all things. The old Alchemist tried to save the situation.

'Surely we can get more feathers in the morning, it can't be impossible.' Jane remembered her treasure.

'Oh look, I've been a complete fool, let me try to make it up to you, here, maybe this will help.' She found Zilp's golden feather and held it out. The Shaman was goggle-eyed, he'd been looking for one of those all his life.

'This is from a fabulous beast, oh red-haired demon.'

'She isn't a demon but I am, sort of,' said Zilp. 'It's one of mine, if they have potency I might be able to spare a couple more,' and he preened obligingly.

'Saints alive, it's a Gryphon cross, I never thought to see one, they're extremely rare!' cried the Shaman with evident glee.

'Well I'm surprised you didn't notice me but nobody introduced us did they? Zilp is my name and I'm not actually a Gryphon-cross but my Aunty Annie Maria was a pure Gryphon, the genes do show.' Zilp picked up two of his feathers which were more like scales and offered them to the Shaman with a warning.

'It is said that if they are used for evil ends the evil returns to the doer a thousand-fold.'

'Would that all evil instruments had the same power,' said the Shaman, thereby commanding respect from all present.

'Well, is that all right then. I'm really sorry I was so hasty,' Jane mumbled, smoothing down her hair. The bacteria colony were very pleased, there is good in lots of bad incidents, usually microscopic.

'Why certainly. All women lose their heads over nothing much at all, they can't help it.' Well, that just showed that she could control herself, for she smiled pleasantly and gave him a kiss. The price of calm added up to quite a bit of sweat and three sorely bitten tongues, but it was time for peace and quiet. Merleau-Ponty thought she would change the subject.

'Have you had news of your girls since we last were together?' she asked Jane. They had gone completely out of her head, she was ashamed – living in the moment was all too easy in this place. She brought Merleau-Ponty up to date on her adventures and the little dog, sensing her distress offered to go there and then and help find them they were obviously in bad company.

'Don't be daft, it is pitch dark and full of snakes outside now, you might just as well be philosophical and stay till day,' advised the Alchemist who had pulled the shutters across Day and lit the lamps against Night while others were busy with their arguments. They all agreed, he was quite right.

'Let's all get stoned,' suggested Merton. Jane felt that she would not mind a change of mood; first a depression, then anger, she needed something, just so long as she didn't get hooked on tobacco again. By this time the Shaman had a nice fat joint rolled. Why did depressions come so quickly and unbidden? Perhaps it was to do with Perpetual Night and Day and the way one faced? Hugh Kolz was already making bannocks and Jane did not want to miss this – they smelled delicious sizzling on the griddle-iron.

The Alchemist's wife administered a few drops of Panacea to those who needed it and the scene became one of total cosiness and rest.

'Man, oh man, but that's real good stuff.' Merton passed the joint to Merleau-Ponty but she politely declined, not approving of dogs smoking. She curled up by the fire and everyone else relaxed too, in perfect peace.

9. Mumbo Jumbo

Jane Saint's bad weather had improved; her depression had entirely gone and indeed everyone seemed happy this morning. She had come to like the old Shaman, he was not a bad old man at all but he had been unable to help with the Quest.

'Where I come from, women are for breeding and work and occasional pleasure, you understand. What else could there be for a female?' The question was so innocently put that Jane hardly knew how to answer.

'We are human beings, with aspirations and longings just like those of men. To ignore this is tragically cruel, it is a persecution of human spirit.'

'But no woman I have ever known has complained of persecution, he replied, performing his morning cleansing ritual, which was blowing his nose.

'Women are just great,' said Merton.

'That is because in your culture women are completely repressed; what you are brought up to believe stays with you except under very strong influence. And perhaps there are punishments for complainers?'

'Of course not, but such a woman would never get herself a husband.' She let it drop, giving him a look which was lost; what was the point of arguing with them one by one, it would take a lifetime and do no good.

The bannocks were delicious and the miraculous smell of bacon and coffee filled the room. She had slept snuggled up with Merleau-Ponty and Zilp all night, a very restful way to sleep, but there was the question of setting off again. The wonderful loving feeling with which she awoke seemed to minimise the problem. If Zilp had been human she could have spent her life with him, she felt, but smiled at herself for even considering a long-term relationship with a male. Zilp was trustworthy and very sympathetic but if he had been human those qualities would have been somewhat diminished, probably. Merton had made something of a pass at her but she had gently put him off, which did not take too much doing as his desire to be perpertually cool severely damaged any real ardour. Hugh had not even thought to kiss her goodnight; if he had any marital rights he must not want to exercise them, thank goodness. Her renewed health would have been spoiled by having to develop a headache!

The Alchemist's wife was making breakfast and Jane saw with interest a very complicated coffee-filter system constructed of retorts and tubes; she hoped they had been well washed for who knew what eye of newt or frightful trituration clung to the glass? Mercury poisoning would not be pleasant. But it smelled divine so she decided to put such thoughts from her. Hot bread was being got from the oven and what with the smell of that and the bacon and the sound of eggs sizzling it was enough to make a hungry soul delirious.

They had taken it in turns to use the oubliette which was a frightening place, and to get washed in a cupboard containing a sink although Merton felt much as the Shaman did about washing, he said that if you removed your outer protective layers of natural oils you were liable to get subtly undermined by cosmic rays. Nobody had proof to the contrary so they did not argue with him.

Jane was wondering if Merleau-Ponty would be sitting up to table with the rest of them but the Alchemist's wife was more practical, she just gave the dog a dish of food and some water by the door knowing perfectly well that even a well-educated dog cannot manage a knife and fork. The others all sat down to a splendid breakfast; Zilp could use a knife and fork excellently because although he had claws he had one opposing just like a thumb, and the inside of his palm was very like that of human beings, giving him great dexterity and a firm but flexible grip. The Shaman did not use cutlery but used only his left hand for eating, quite the opposite of some religious practice.

'My goodness but that was splendid, thank you – do you always eat as well as this?' said Hugh, gratefully appreciating a meal that would not have disgraced a High Table at some illustrious college.

'Not when he cooks it, we share the work here, because we work in Yin Yang principle and turn and turn about.'

'Ay well, maybe you don't do as well as me in the making of Anthroparion,' said the Alchemist defensively.

'No, but I've yet to see you complete the Work,' she retorted gently.

'Well I'm very glad you failed last night because there would have been no hole in time and space for me to slip through – this has been one of my pleasanter visits, on the whole.' Jane blushed at the Shaman's words.

.'Yes and I wouldn't have got here either and met Jane and I'm very glad about that,' said Zilp, finishing off with a bit of toast and marmalade. So that was all right, but the Alchemist and his wife were pledged to their task and repeating the experiment. The Shaman got a little bottle with blue crystals in it to dissolve in tea for the Chief's daughter, and he asked what he could do in return.

'We'll think of something when need be,' they told him.

Hugh Kolz cleared his throat. 'I would like to put myself forward for consideration as an apprentice here if you have a vacancy. I do believe that this is just what I have been looking for.' Everyone was very surprised except the Alchemist and his wife who smiled little smiles; they had been expecting this. Merton looked a bit put out, he was an apprentice of sorts and feared being displaced, but Jane's heart leapt – she could get rid of Hugh without a quarrel, if that was what he wanted then she could go on without him and his oppressive atmosphere. It never even occurred to her that her husband had publicly announced his intention of leaving her without consulting her first.

Hugh Kolz was accepted instantly, so Jane got up from the table, offering to wash the dishes but it was the old man's turn, they didn't let visitors wash dishes, thanks all the same. Merleau-Ponty said she would like to travel with Jane again, and Zilp's allegiance was not in question, he was holding her hand ready to go. Jane thanked everyone for the hospitality and company and the old couple said maybe she would be visiting again?

'I doubt it somehow but if I do I shall be very glad.'

Hugh shook hands with the three travellers but had no suitable words. She gave the Shaman a kiss and he grabbed her bottom in a friendly feel, obviously rather regretful that she was not a dallying demon. She checked that she had the capsule and was alarmed to find that it glowed in the darkness at the bottom of her rucksack. Radioactive? Too late to worry.

And so they left, and walked together over the hot plain for a long time without looking back, and were beginning to be tired when the weather changed; a mist arose and it became considerably cooler.

Soon they were walking over peat with gorse and heather and gritty rocks strewn about.

'This mist is bad for my arthritis,' said Merleau-Ponty.

'Have you got arthritis, love?' – Jane was concerned.

'Well I feel things in my bones anyway.' There were shadows in the mist and Jane, too, began to sense something. There was a stink in the air, of rotting vegetation like a mere gone stagnant, then they could hear bubbling.

'Better be careful, might be boggy,' said Jane.

Merleau-Ponty clearly did not like it at all, she drew back in trepidation, whimpering.

'I don't think it's anything to worry about,' said Zilp, grinning in recognition – I think we've found an old friend of mine.' Merleau-Ponty stood set, hair raised.

'As I thought. Jane, meet Agatha Hardcastle, the Witch of Heptonstall.' Jane was very impressed indeed when an ancient woman, wearing not a stitch of clothing, with grey hair like etiolated steel wool came shuffling up out of the mist to greet them, clutching a large teacup in her gnarled hands. There was a cave behind her, at its opening a cauldron bubbled over a fire. It had odours coming from it; exactly what one would expect a witch's cauldron to smell like. The woman smiled in greeting, displaying occasional teeth; she was gloriously warty and her legs were knobbly everywhere that legs should not be.

The beautiful ageless woman and the hideous aged woman regarded one another each recognising another self.

'Agatha, meet Jane Saint.' Agatha flashed some kind of look sufficing for social behaviour and Jane extended a hand which was ignored while the witch looked into her eyes. She was apparently not displeased.

'I suppose you think, young lady, that I can help you with some problem. I suppose it's a man, it usually is.'

'Not a man, but men and women. I'm trying to change human consciousness so that womankind may be free as man.'

The cackling that greeted this speech was a delight to the ear. Pure humour! Oh, very funny! Ironic, cynical and gleeful laughter all at once. Some foul liquid spilled from her cup and sizzled on the ground and little newtlike creatures sprang from it, running away squealing.

'Womankind is freer than mankind already, little one. We have the power of creation, the hand that rocks the cradle and so on . . .'

'Oh no, not *that*,' moaned Jane desperately, having heard it all too often. Use your charm, manipulate men, get power by stealth – it was a way to survive and exert influence but it was also enforced dishonesty, and it ruled out friendship with men. She grasped Zilp's claw for strength, frustrated tears were on the way.

'I would have thought, Madam, that you would have acquired greater wisdom than that kind of glib trash . . .'

'Just testing,' muttered the witch with more cackling. 'Just testing at what stage you are. So many women come to me wanting freedom and it turns out all they want is more housekeeping money from their husbands – more bondage in fact.' Jane had to cackle a bit now for the crone had style and wit. The chains of so-called easy money – no thanks, something a bit different from that.

'But be sure you want your independence, Jane Saint, before you leap. It is a great responsibility to saddle all womankind with freedom before they are ready for it. Most have no way to earn a living once the head of the household is gone.' True.

'I want to make it possible for them to survive; when a thing is impossible the spirit is choked and cannot develop – if a thing is possible, people will work for it.' The old witch clearly understood and agreed with this.

'Well then, I can brew up just the potion you need. It will make you see everything differently once you have drunk it – you will have a different viewpoint.'

'But that's like a man saying to a woman that "it is all in the mind" – you know, with a female problem, some men think it's all imagination.'

'Just testing. Okay okay, I'll do what you really want. I'll brew up a real potion, a super-strength trituration which you will have to get into all the world's water supply, which will totally change the masculine viewpoint.' That was like women telling men that 'it was all in the mind' – but then, it was, wasn't it? And besides

76

there was already the capsule for the Thought Library which was designed to do as much. She told Agatha about this.

'Bah – that's new-fangled electronics and brain chemistry and suchlike – useless. What you need is old-fashioned herbal remedies, my dear. There's nobody can do this except myself, in fact I don't know why I haven't thought of it before. Probably because I don't sodding well care, I'm getting too old.' She turned and went into the cave and started messing about with gruesome things on the floor and Jane saw to her astonishment that something was added from a large jar marked 'Parsley'. Of course, you can't judge a content by its label. Agatha crouched, grinding things with a pestle and mortar, her great flanks wobbling. Jane and Zilp looked at one another, Jane in doubt, Zilp in triumph.

'This is exactly what you need Jane, her remedies never fail.' He looked very pleased.

'You can trust Agatha you know.' Jane was not certain, how much of an anarchist was she – enough to doctor the water supply? She was already here courtesy of being in custody, how could she accomplish it without going back?

'It feels like pushing my luck,' she told him quietly.

'You never do anything else but push your luck!' True, it was almost a way of life now.

'But is it ethical to put things in the water supply?' she next asked, really pushing her luck for the old witch overheard her and almost chucked out the potion and sent her customers packing. But she had patience, she wanted Jane to have the potion and find a way to use it. War was war – ethics didn't come into it and the potion would do less damage to the world than leaving things to go on the way they were. Someone had once told Agatha 'there, my little love, just sit and look beautiful, don't bother your head about a thing' – and then changed their tune as Agatha changed with age: she had not forgotten. Her head had its uses, as ever.

'Jane, I've been thinking.' This was Merleau-Ponty who had kept out of the proceedings. 'I think I'll have to be on my way.' Leave? Before the end of the Quest? But they had become companions. Jane was desolate and Zilp could not understand why.

'I can't take all this mumbo-jumbo, Jane. It's my training, I can't help it – I prefer dialectic, discussion, democracy, legislation – I'm afraid magic leaves me very unimpressed as a political tool,' said the little dog in some distress.

'But magic is more that its name implies,' began Zilp.

'I daresay, please don't think I've just fallen into a semantic trap. But firstly I don't think it will work, and secondly if I am wrong and it does work, it won't suddenly turn men into being compassionate about women, it is going to fucking well poison them – have you seen what she's putting into that stuff?' Parsley?

'Unless I am mistaken there was the liver of a dog which had been crucified at the dark of the moon, buried at a crossroads and dug up at full moon, and other things I would rather not go into. I am not ignorant of the subject.'

Obviously. And it was evident that her mind was decided – she was leaving.

'I shall miss you very much. Let's hope that we meet again some day, say that at least.'

'We'll meet again some day.' Jane, risking toxicaria, kissed her friend ardently and the little red-haired dog went trotting off, away from the despised cave. Jane began to feel awkward – perhaps her friend was right? While they were waiting for the potion to brew she took a look around. They were at the foot of a crag, and the slimy bog bubbled occasionally, making inviting and obscene sucking noises. It smelled awful but looked like spinach soup. Zilp whispered something to Jane which she could not catch. Mm? He shook his head – not to let the witch hear. She bent to him, and Zilp told her that the witch would want payment. Crumbs! never thought of that. What would she want? Jane rummaged through the rucksack, there wasn't anything valuable.

But Agatha had overheard. 'I shall want twenty pieces of freshly made gold, or I'll have Zilp as a hostage. He's worked for me before, haven't you, pet?' Zilp told Jane that he had, and liked the work, he would be quite willing to stay until she could get the payment. Only the Alchemist could help her with that sort of payment and she did not want to retrace her steps. It was out of the question that Zilp be left as hostage.

'I can't take the potion then, I haven't the price.'

'I've said – I'll stay, I don't mind except of course I shall miss you for a while.' Knowing what 'while' could mean in a Timeless zone, Jane was not enthusiastic.

'But supposing I fail to get back with the gold what then?'

'You are resourceful and lucky, it'll be okay.'

'There's never a guarantee.' She would have to cancel the order, she was very sorry.

'The order's completed, you have to have it,' said Agatha sourly.

'No I don't, somebody else might buy it or perhaps you could alter it for another purpose? I didn't promise to take it, did I?'

'You should never argue with a witch,' Agatha muttered glowering, her chin setting up firm. 'I shall throw this potion into the bog in a moment if you don't make up your mind and then you have lost your chance.'

'Everything is against my having that potion now Agatha Hardcastle, I should feel to be betraying my friend even if he is willing.' Agatha held the small bottle up.

'If your Quest is that important, what is one Zilp more or less – your sense of values is screwy,' said Agatha, and in a sudden lurch of bad temper she threw the potion up towards the morass. Now Jane did not like that kind of unwholesome reasoning, and when at school she had been a whizz fielder at baseball, and her reflexes made her leap, one arm outstretched, and she caught the vial just before it touched the slime. But she lost her balance, and screaming, which is the one thing you should not do when being immersed in mud, she was sucked into the bog. She heard someone say: 'You idiot you've let the water level rise again, if she drowns that'll be the end of us here' and felt Zilp's claws holding her hair and her pullover but the sucking power of the muddy stuff was immense, she felt like spaghetti being consumed by a hungry mouth.

The last sound she heard, accompanied by flashing lights and a

terrible roaring in her ears, was the cackling of Agatha
Hardcastle, Witch of Heptonstall.

10. In the Nick of Time

The noise was appalling. Not only in her ears, there was
screaming, whirring. She could breathe again, and bring up her
hands to wipe her eyes, and look up towards the noise to see the
helicopter again, hauling in a trussed but fiercely protesting Zilp.
The door closed and the mist swallowed sight and sound. She
spat the foul bog out of her mouth and wondered why they had
taken Zilp and why they had not taken her? Perhaps they had
been after her but not been able to see her – she blended into her
background perfectly whereas she had seen Zilp's golden scales –
and where was Agatha Hardcastle?

Mysteries – but this was a different place; she must have gone
right through the bog, far down, a two-sided bog? Miraculously,
she still had the vial clutched in her left hand like a straw. What
next?

There was a thundering of hooves over firm turf and a
mounted horse pulled up, rearing and neighing, the rider clad in
armour and carrying a pennant bearing the words: 'Revenge
Advances'. This whole presence was most alarming as anyone
who has seen a mounted horse closeup from a prone position will
readily recall.

'Good day woman, why do you roll in mud – are you slimming
or something?'

'I seem to have come right through it, rescued by my friend
but he was captured just as I was recovering my wits. Do you
know a place I can bathe?'

'I do, and not far. A stream with a waterfall, get up behind me and I'll take you.'

'I'm too filthy . . .'

'No matter, I'll bathe too, wearing armour is monstrous hot. And who are you and what were you doing in Freud's Tide?'

'I am Jane Saint and I am here on a Quest on behalf of women. I always thought Freud's Tide was black mud, but this is green. And who are you?' The visor was still down concealing all clues.

'I don't suppose Freud had actually seen it when he spoke of it, he lacked vision. I am Joan of Arc.'

Jane was awestruck. Really? She made known her pleasure and admiration in some confusion. A kindred spirit in many ways.

'Jane, I am searching for Warwick, can you give me any directions?'

'Well not from here but it's right in the centre of England, not two miles from Leamington Spa which was built long after your time. Madame Tussaud owns Warwick Castle; now, it makes a pleasant day out, although the Torture Chamber is grisly. There's a sort of iron basket there where they used to hang men in chains to die, it must have been awful . . .'

'We misunderstand. Warwick. The Earl of Warwick.' Oh. Sorry no. Crumbs, that was tactless about the torture chamber. Never was much good at historic detail. Joan seemed a little worried but urged Jane to scramble up behind her, and they galloped off, a fine sensation and new to Jane who had never ridden a horse. It would be nice to have her girls go to riding school, all girls were supposed to like horses. But first, find the girls.

Joan slowed the horse and shouted back to Jane, asking her what she intended to do for women. Jane told her everything briefly not confident of being understood.

'I wish you luck. If I had been a man they would have listened and not deemed me witch. I am on an avenging mission. When I find Warwick I intend to make an example of him maybe threaten to burn him alive to see how he likes it but of course I won't really. Sometimes, of course, I'd really like to burn the bastard – or hang him alive in chains, I can't help it.' They fetched up by a deep stream of clear water and Jane stripped off and washed her clothes, then draped them on some blackberry bushes to dry in the sun and breeze. Then she plunged in yelping with the cold shock and turned to Joan, suddenly filled with a powerful dread of what she might see of Joan underneath her armour. But the saint's flesh had been made whole, this was no charred horror but a normal strong young woman with extremely short pale hair with a Fleur-de-Lys dyed into it at the back, in vivid green. Jane got out again to rinse her rucksack, fortunately not much mud had seeped inside. She considered pouring Agatha's potion away but her canny side said to keep it with the other bits and pieces, which she did. Then she plunged in again holding a handful of grasses to scrub herself clean.

The place was very pleasant with woodland around and sun streaming through the branches, dimly recalling some movie that Jane had seen about a Holy Grail and a snake – must have been symbolic. The two women swam and dashed in and out of the waterfall, playing like children and filled with an unbidden love for one another in accord with the moment.

When they felt too chilled, they got out and ran through the wood to get warm, and then breathlessly sat by the water, refreshed. They discussed the capsule and the potion, and Joan said that she should not trust in such things without checking; she never had trusted blindly in anything except God, and quite frankly she was getting a bit pissed off with him – he had begun to say such daft things to her that her faith was shaken.

'I more than half think the voices were in my own head after all. I didn't want to be martyred though – nobody in their right mind would.' Quite. Jane filled her in about the Revolutionaries. 'I'm dubious, Jane. This is War and there will be traitors within our ranks. I advise great caution.' They were agreed upon that but time was short; although this place was Timeless by earth standards, Jane had a feeling that her earth-time was running out – if she got back too late it would be into a brain she did not recognise. These thoughts brought Jane down from her inflated mood.

'What shall I do? I don't feel equal to my task.'

'I think you will be ready when the time comes and it will be soon. Do not despair. Once I would have said pray to God for guidance but not now – how I have wished that God was female.'

'If she had been, the whole world would be quite different. No. We are on our own, it is all up to us. Not very cheering thoughts but it did imply activity rather than passivity.

'If you eliminate the male totally and there is a God, then she will be female.' Wild speculation.

'I've got to go, which way do you advise?'

'I can set you down by the right place, I know the building well. I hate it the way it overshadows everything else, I wouldn't want to go inside.' They got dressed again, mounted the horse who had taken his fill of water and been choosing the best bits of grass to munch, and rode off out of the woods and over a plain. It was not far. Joan put her down and then bent low from her saddle, lifting her visor to give her friend a parting kiss.

And then she was gone in the thunder of hooves and light flashing off her armour, a splendid sight. Lonely sainthood, isolated martyrdom. Would that be her own fate in the end? Was she willing? Better leave that question to await a practical proof.

The Thought Library was so tall that the top seemed to go up to a point in the sky, and it was a vast structure at its base, all shiny black and squared and sparse with no windows. The front doors slid open as she approached and closed behind her. The air was warm and there was a slight humming sound. There were elevator doors with a staggering number of floors to choose from, and a console which flickered words at her: Preliminary enquiry: please state business. She approached it very nervously but the directions for use were very clear. There were little lighted squares to touch, much like on some car-park meters, with several information keys. Layer of consciousness if known. Historic time: millenium, century, decade and so on. Planetary area, Classification of thought – there were fifty basic types for a start! Name of individual, if relevant. And then, reason for enquiry. Oh dear, just for taking things out, not for input. But she had directions written down, Jane looked through her rucksack for them. The piece of paper was damp and dirty now, she could not read it – but what was the other console? Input. Special case only. Ah.

Nothing here except to speak the request clearly. She hesitated, self-conscious at recording her voice, she had always loathed answering systems and could never speak to them without first having written down her speech.

She also profoundly mistrusted the whole atmosphere, this futuristic setting was far more spooky to her than any Gothic mansion. She paced slowly, considering, and her bare foot trod upon some small thing; it was a wilted buttercup. She knelt over it full of wonder at finding a living thing besides herself in this place, perhaps she had brought it in with her without knowing? It recalled her girls playing in a meadow, weaving crowns of these, daisies and some flower like hemlock, called Motherdie.

Then she was aroused by sounds, alert, and the elevator doors opened and out rushed her girls hauling bicycles, giggling and screaming as happy girls will. They never noticed Jane who joyfully watched them mount their bicycles and start to race around the great hall, until they heard their mother call, then bikes were flung and screeches rang and what chattering broke out like a cataract of monkeys with the gift of tongues.

'Yes Mummy, a super old Shaman came and rescued us from the nasty men. We knew you'd come here, they told us so, but we didn't know how long.'

'Mum, you should have seen the Shaman zap with his fists, he said he was just getting into violence and that you'd taught him how that can't be right.'

'Darling Ma, we've been getting an education here: Daddy gave us a syllabus, and Anthroparion told him where this was; we come and get stuff out and get wired up and it goes in like a dream better than school.'

'But the Shaman couldn't get Zilp, they'd got him in solitary under guard. They locked us up for a while and put us in these awful clothes.' They were wearing a very plain school uniform with heavy black shoes and white knee-socks.

'They braided our hair so tight it hurt, but we undid it. They got tired of doing it up again. Mum, they were awful people.' Whatever Jane said to them did not match her profound feelings but all four knew their eternal love and were renewed by this reunion.

'So what is this schooling?' the mother enquired of her children.

'I'm doing advanced computer tech. and general subjects and three languages,' Melanie said, pushing back her dark hair and looking for approval with fathomless eyes.

'I'm doing micro-electronics and brain chemistry and music and one extra language.' Dolores' milky skin blushed to hide its freckles, her crinkly hair flaming paler than her mother's, her light grey eyes very clear.

'And I'm doing astrophysics and human metabolism and general subjects and two extra languages,' Sybil proudly announced, her cool blue eyes shining and her blonde hair as straight as the shortest distance between two points. 'But we are all doing an intensive short-course on information storage because Daddy said that we might need it. We are living with the Alchemist and his wife, he's very sweet, he's a secret knitter, he does Fair-Isle like a dream and she tells wonderful stories from memory in the evenings by the fire.'

'And they've got a cat, you didn't know, did you? He's very fluffy black with some white bits underneath and he's called Mr Rochester. He's not always there, he goes off on trips of his own, nobody knows where.'

'Come and see the work-space we've been allotted.' As they all crowded into the elevator with one of the bicycles Jane asked where they got these rather flashy bikes from; apparently a real Anthroparian had come and they'd asked him and he'd told them where there was a bike shop and as a special concession the Alchemist had made them some gold to spend rather than throw out, there were twelve gears and a dynamo and lots of other exciting details.

'Well, now I must have my turn to speak.' Jane told them about the capsule. As they all got out of the elevator their whole mood had changed; they were alert and serious.

'We've got to check it out Ma, it sounds dangerous.'

'This is where our short-course comes in handy.' They all thought that the building itself would somehow have attempted to stop her project – she had to get it in the right place without enquiry, it was a matter of the overwhelming sum total of human feeling being against such a major change. It needed thinking through. Jane thought to herself that the fact that women had allowed themselves to be conned out of thousands of years of equality and freedom was sufficient to make anyone think that they actually *were* really inferior!

'Mummy, it will take us a little while to analyse this capsule.' She was stunned at the educational leaps they had taken with these methods; Hugh had done well for them. She had a brief vision of her girls uneducated, which if nothing changed they might well be – chained in eternal drudgery or brainwashed into things unthinkable. The project must succeed. It was obviously right that her girls should be here, she could not have succeeded alone, nor without Hugh it now seemed.

They had the use of something resembling an electron microscope, and she watched them work as a team and was unable to be of any use.

'This capsule dear Ma, is dynamite!' muttered Sybil, going over the first readings. 'Yeah, it says here more or less what you were told. This will influence things to the extent that it will seem as if the male never happened. Now this seems to me like a trick.'

'Which trick?'

'Well, so far, we haven't had much parthogenesis, right? If there had never been males there would have been no human world at all, the way I see it?'

It was a skullbreaking possibility – could the entire universe as existing in human thought depend upon a linguistic cockup? In the beginning – and it all depends upon which word.

'We must modify it. Not easy but possible. How?'

'Who gave you this?'

'Sort of old-time communist cell types.'

'Sound like they weren't after women's liberation but Armageddon.'

'They were probably archetypal anarchists. Chaos at any price.' All too likely. But perhaps they could help Jane Saint whether they intended it or not.

'How come they could achieve this capsule?'

'They said their scientists were very advanced.' The girls laughed, 'Russians' always claimed that. They were like destructive spirits in disguise, in Sybil's opinion it was a massive stroke of luck that the capsule had not been inserted without modification.

They all discussed possible modification without much misunderstanding or disagreement. The girls were thinking for themselves, Jane was proud to notice, and not merely repeating things she had put before them. Melanie gave them all a scare by observing that everything they were thinking must be recorded by the building.

'Yes, but it won't be noticed until somebody asks for the reference, the building isn't a being.' They profoundly hoped that it did not have a motivated consciousness but only possible defences down in the entrance hall.

'Mummy, I think you look tired and quite frankly now we've got it sorted out I think you should take a rest while we finish the work.' She acquiesced gratefully, satisfied that their solution would be adequate.

Basically all that was needed was a slight altering of the fuse of intelligence and some extra capacity for compassion, which they agreed that everyone could use but this was with special reference to the matter in hand. That and more important alterations would have the power to entirely change the world and the relationship between sexes. They even thought it possible that there could be legislation to aid the cause, and that men would not criminally evade those laws, as hitherto.

Jane wandered off for a brief respite, hoping that at the top of the building there might be access to fresh air. The conditioned air in the place was as false as conditioned people. The elevator journey was rapid and nauseating filling her with claustrophobia and doubts. Supposing the capsule didn't fit at all? Ha ha bloody ha. Hope. Eternal hope. Hope of the world. That's all there is during a respite. So.

But the doors opened and there was air, uncannily without the howling wind which she had half expected. There was a large roof-garden containing many varieties of extinct plant. Jane, who collected houseplants, was already wondering if it would be stealing to take a few cuttings; they were very interesting. The more primitive the plant, the more human qualities it seemed to have, a remarkable fact which perhaps Darwin had not noticed?

Meanwhile, the girls were making headway. They almost had the job finished and heard Jane returning. And yet not Jane for her feet were bare and silent, this was a clicking. Canine claws pattering rapidly on obdurate black floors is what they heard, and in scurried Merleau-Ponty in a hell of a hurry and panting, listen: 'Where's Jane, Zilp is in danger, he won't tell them, but it is awful what they are doing, but Volto is a traitor, you see, he's so well trained. Listen, I can hardly speak I ran so fast, they're following me – they're onto your plot, the whole lot of them, the pilot, he's got them together.' She rolled over onto her side, this little red-haired overbred beast, all her heart working on every level to get this message through. People should not despise pedigree dogs; have there been no good aristocrats, come on now, honest Injun?

'Oh poor little dog, take it easy, we're listening.'

'Which pilot? You mean the nasty man?'

'Yes. That one, Acrid von Sturmundrang. He had got all the forces of darkness together against her – all the male ones that is.' She was just about all in and, speeding, she could have written a book right now but speak dog speak.

'They can fuck the whole thing up. They will make her permanent here, she'll go on like this for Eternity, never accomplishing anything. And you three also.' What could they do to Jane?

'Water.' While Sybil took the bike to look for Jane, Dolores took Merleau-Ponty to the washroom and Melanie concentrated on completion of the capsule. It required some extremely delicate laser eliding and then very tricky insertion of already prepared material.

Sybil zoomed down to reception to ask enquiries where Jane was, but it announced itself 'Temporarily Out of Service' which was unheard of, therefore sinister. She got her bike and rushed around a floor at a time screeching around corners but realised her method was too slow and just a matter of luck which seemed to be running out.

In the washroom a revived Merleau-Ponty explained further.

'They will take all her life's thoughts and everything thought about her and put them in some obsolete sub-section, then construct yet another version of the Red-haired Heroine, make it seem ludicrous, and pop it into the Occasional Archetypal Nightdream section. It's that simple, apparently it has been done before, for example with the Suffragettes. The method makes people forget that the movement was ever about something *real*.'

They went together back to the workspace but Melanie had gone. Had they got her? Or had she gone to insert the completed capsule?

Meanwhile Sybil was just deciding to return to that workspace room. Merleau-Ponty and Dolores headed for Central Id, where the only slot in the building where major reprogramming could take place waited. Why was it there? They did not know, but perhaps there was something deep within the human Id which desired such a space? There was Melanie at the far end of the corridor, running in her heavy shoes; they followed, calling, and she waved in triumph briefly holding up the all-important egg-like object.

The doors of the room slid back silently revealing a perfectly formed young blond male in immaculate uniform having difficulty staying upright in unmercifully polished jackboots.

'Hantsup! Giff zat kepsule to me!' There was a two seconds silence. Merleau-Ponty sprang like a frog on heroin right for his throat just as Melanie blew him a very dirty raspberry and ran right past him. He dropped his gun just as he fired into the wall which bounced the bullet off with chilling echoes all down the corridor and the gun hit the floor spinning towards Dolores who did a nose-dive, her fair hand mirrored under it as she grabbed it and sprang upright just as she had learned to do in the gym. Not a quiver from head to toe, footwear unsuitable as it was.

Melanie punched out the opening sequences cool as ice and the cover of the slot opened like an automatic till at a bank. She said:

> Computer Good, Computer Bright,
> Take this data and make things Right.

She held out the capsule to place it in the slot. Merleau-Ponty fell back from the man's throat and he sent her flying with his jackboot under her belly and easily twisted the gun out of the agile but not very strong girl's hand: he shot Melanie in the back and blood fountained everywhere running like mercury on that everlasting blackness, precious droplets dancing to the music of female screams.

Meanwhile on the roof garden, Jane explored. When she looked over the extremely low parapet she could not see the ground and drew back sweating with fear. She was about to sit down with her back to the wall when she heard the approaching helicopter. It circled round, the door opened.

Then a wonderful thing happened. Zilp flew out, his wings stretched, floating and flapping towards her. She ran to greet him full of love and joy, overcome with delight at yet another reunion, her friend returned. As she stood, the plants were twining tendrils round her and she had to disentangle her rucksack to run forward calling his name, her arms open.

But Zilp fell stone-like, landed at her feet a relief sculpture of himself, not flying but dying, already dead. Vitriol smoked on the marble. This must be the most awful moment of her life.

She ran this way and that, distraught, crying. Dreadful criminals. Wicked murderers. If this was a result of trying to change the world then it was not worth it – her dearest friend martyred. She returned to his body and found a note tied to one claw.

'He wouldn't talk but others have. You are finished. We are coming to get you.' The helicopter circled, menacing. Jane could see that Zilp had been tortured, she touched his golden feathers and they clicked gently to the floor. She gathered a few and put them into her rucksack, not as treasure but as a remembrance. She averted her eyes from the mutilated form which revealed so much human skin beneath. Revenge stirred within her.

Now, she did not want to abandon the Quest but to intensify it; whoever had done this must be outwitted.

Sobbing, she headed for the elevator door and the helicopter closed in showering flaming arrows. She dodged and whirled and still they came aiming at Jane Saint, the terrible arrows of some vile desire.

'You can't succeed woman, it is too late. You shall be put in your place!' came the voice from the loud-hailer.

'Yes, I will succeed,' her voice carried into the din. 'Now I shall succeed; you have given me strength!' and she shook her fist at the voice running at it madly, her hair alight.

She ran into a parapet and hurtled over it falling like the darting flames around her, a rain of fire into the vortex of rushing wind sucking down into fearful darkness and her screams were lost.

The capsule fell from Melanie's shocked hand into the waiting slot and the cover slid back; the man gunned the cover with futile shots, leaving it unmarked until his ammunition was spent, for only a perfect code could open such an orifice. Then dog and girl fought man with all the fury that they knew.

When Jane Saint opened her eyes, she was completely bewildered. A man and woman in white overalls were rubbing her with soft towels in a stream of warm air. She noticed the pads of her fingers had gone white and wrinkled and for a few moments she looked around for her rubber Donald Duck and the wooden nailbrush which was a sailing ship.

'Shall we tell her?' said one nurse to the other. Jane gazed at them uncomprehendingly for their voices were kind. She began to remember very quickly. This must be part of the brainwashing.

'You have been pardoned. Jane. It is all right.' She did not believe them, these people lied all the time.

'It's true,' said the man looking into her eyes, and she could see compassion there, delight in another's freedom. She had never seen that look in the eyes of a man before, it seemed alien and not to be trusted.

'Come and rest for a while, your things are here when you feel like getting dressed, ring if you need help.'

'What about my girls?'

'They are waiting for you, but one of them has been ill. She is almost recovered but has had pneumonia, she got water in her lungs with a little internal bleeding, but she has been well looked after. Dolores and Sybil are fine and are keeping her company.'

'Pardoned?' But they left her then, smiling.

Her body hardly felt to belong to her at first, but curiosity and the desire to see her girls gave her strength and co-ordination, and she pulled her rucksack over and looked inside. Her clothes were there, her jeans and her personal tee-shirt with her name on it and clean underwear and some rather scruffy sneakers. There were other things in the rucksack. A funny old Fair-Isle pullover with frizzled burns on it, a pair of men's Y-front pants with a huge safety pin in the waistband.

A mirror with blood dried on it, a bottle of Guinness, one or two other bits and pieces. A funny little bottle sealed with wax and a label obscured by sticky green dust. She scratched and revealed words: Do not ye open thysse lest sore need be. And thirteen exquisite golden feathers, now catching her tears. If only Zilp had been able to come back with her, if only he too could be reborn as perhaps she was.

Was it true that the world was going to be a place for all to have a chance to be glad to be alive in after all? Had the girls successfully placed the capsule and was it effective? Had laws been changed? Had attitudes changed overnight? The male nurse returned as she was finishing dressing.

'Have you got a bottle-opener by any chance?' she enquired. He had one on a key-ring and opened her bottle. They shared it, frothy though it was for it had been hurtled rapidly, not good for any bottled beer.

'Come on Jane, let me help you walk, you need some proper food and to be with your girls. But first, the sisters are waiting outside to see you.' He opened the window to let in the sound of cheering.

Woe, Blight
and, in Heaven, Laughs

Lucille hated her stepmother. Most people hated Lucille's stepmother; she was a crabby bitch. But then, most people hated most people anyway. The world was not happy. There were personal reasons why Lucille hated her stepmother, and a personal reason why the old bitch hated Lucille. Lucille hated the older woman because Lucille had tried and completely failed to love her, and this was galling and, besides, the older woman was horrid to her. The stepmother hated the girl because they were both beautiful, with raven hair, lily-white skin, and scarlet lips and rosy cheeks. The lips and cheeks were paint, but the rest was for real. It could have been that time was on the side of Lucille, but unfortunately, she had not long to live. She had a slow form of leukaemia, difficult to cure even if there had been any proper medical services, and this accounted for the fragile and translucent nature of her skin, and her habit of lying around the apartment all day, sighing. The older woman was not full of sympathy and understanding; she was frankly jealous. The men around the place quite obviously preferred Lucille in spite of her lack of energy, but Lucille rejected them all. She did not want a pregnancy if she was going to die; there were few contraceptives of any kind even on the black market and anyway most of the men were not offering love, but money.

Lucille's father was dead from repeated overdoses of various drugs of the kind that cause people to think that the world is not in a terrible mess, and had left his second wife, Queenie, and his daughter, his beloved Lucille, without any money. Lucille had added very little to the income; she did not like selling herself. There were very few other jobs for women, and those there were usually had extra night duties of the kind Lucille wished to avoid. Queenie thought this unwillingness on the part of her step-daughter snobbish and selfish, which, seen in some lights, it was. Lucille dreamed of a healthy handsome fellow who would love her, make her feel well again. Her most outright fantasies included a beautiful doctor with a miracle cure for her leukaemia. But she knew that this was nonsense. Queenie thought it downright mad. She went into her private cubicle, and switched on her Frend.

'I'd like to ask a few questions. I need a confidence boost.' She swiftly programmed it, and onto the small screen came a Frendly face wreathed in understanding smiles. Queenie put her question.

'Who is the most beautiful woman for miles around? Who has the most sexual attraction, the nicest figure, the blackest hair and the most energy? I know the answers but I need to hear you say it.' The Frend was working well, and it answered: 'You are, Queenie. You are, of course, have no doubt. You are unbeatable for your age; you'll be getting fellas when Lucille is ashes and dust.' That was fine. But what did it mean 'for her age'? Huh?

'How do you mean, "for my age"?' The Frend went dark. Damn. Have to get it serviced. Not an easy matter, getting gadgets serviced. It was not like in Queenie's childhood when it would have been a simple matter to call a repair man. Now, you had to have influence and money, and know where to ask, to get things done. The whole economic structure was wobbly; people just didn't care any more; workmen were so sloppy. Blast. Still, it had said that she was the most beautiful. That was better than nothing, for who else would say it?

She went back into the communal cubicle and spent the rest of the afternoon combing her hair, trying not to notice how much was coming out in the comb (fallout, no joke) and picking on Lucille to try to get her to quarrel. But the girl was not competitive, she didn't like quarreling. It was sometimes called being sweet-natured, or once had been. 'Sweet-natured, my ass, she's just trying to provoke me further,' thought Queenie. Lucille noticed after a while how horrid her stepmother was being, and knew that she ought to try and quarrel a bit because it kept the old girl quiet, so to speak. At least she did not start physical assault if the bickering was interesting enough. But the frail girl felt so tired, and could not even sleep with that noise going on.

'I'm sorry, Queenie. I can't help it. You are the best-looking, you always have been. I don't know what you are worrying about. All that crap about Father marrying you just because we are the spittin' image of each other, it's time you forgot that. He didn't like me so much, he used to beat me. You know you'll always get fellas. I can't get fellas, I've no zing.'

'You're only saying that, you little cow. You know you are lazy, and a snob, you think you are above the street, you are just too high and mighty, acting like an old-time princess. You don't do anything, you just live off my earnings.'

'What's a cow, Queenie?' There was an uninformed silence. The girl continued. 'I'd get a job, but the job situation is terrible. You know that. Besides, I am sick. I'll be out of your way soon enough.' One could of course go and work Underground; it might be possible to get Queenie to pull a few strings. But people never returned from there. They lived down there and did not return for visits. It was the food that did it. They went mad from eating good food that was grown down there for consumption up top, and rumour had it that they could eat all they wanted of hydroponic melons, cresses, radishes. Stuff that was a very great luxury, and very rare up top. But it was some decision, to go where you would never see the light of day again? Not that you saw it much anyway, what with all the thick clouds, low and greenish most days.

'Let me comb your hair, Queenie, I'll make it nice and smooth.' Keep in with her. She often threatened to throw the girl out but hadn't yet. To die on the street was much worse than dying here, even with Queenie being so unpleasant.

'Oh, shut up, girl! You'll pull it all out, that's a fact. You want to disfigure me?' It wasn't fair. Nothing she could do was right. Lucille lay back and shut her eyes. Two tears oozed out from between her lids. Queenie saw, and screeched with rage. Crying to get sympathy! She threw the comb, then the brush, then herself. Lucille got out into her own cubicle but not without a few bruises that would never heal. Not where they showed, though. That was something.

It was when the Frend went berserk on her that Queenie too got out of hand, and flipped completely. The machine had told her straight to her face that Lucille was better looking that she was, and that she herself was a crabby, mean, old woman. She did not keep the Frend to tell the truth! She would have Lucille wiped out, once and for all. True, she was dying anyway, but it would take time, maybe as much as a year or more, and time was short for everyone, like as not. She would not do the thing herself, but get Gordy Hunter to do it for her. He loved killings. He would accept money and a few favours in return for the job. Not here in the apartment, though. Outside somewhere. Getting Lucille out of the apartment would not be easy, she almost never went out. She could perhaps stage a love affair between Lucille and Gordy; get Lucille at least interested enough to go out with him. Gordy would like to play a game like that, it would tickle his imagination to see Lucille falling for him, and then kill her. He was like that. Queenie had acquired several rather extreme friends in her trade, and sometimes they came in useful. Black market contacts, fences, drug-pushers for things like aspirin and antibiotics. But this would be the first time she had hired a killer. It was exciting . . .

One day Gordy arrived at the apartment and during his visit he started talking real nice to Lucille. It took five such visits to get her to go out with him and he saw her four more times after that, each time taking her a little further out of town. He talked about all the things that interested her, and discovered her fantasies, and did not sneer at them. He said that he wished he were a medical man so that he could cure her. He also wished that he was handsome and healthy. Lucille kindly said that he was handsome. She had begun to fall for him, for during all this time he had not once assumed that she was his, and forced her, physically. It was not that she had no sexual feelings; it was the sheer novelty of a fella taking her for a person, rather than a thing.

They were out on the mudflats one night watching a circular effulgence that was a full moon behind the permanent smoke-screen, when Gordy Hunter got out his knife and grabbed Lucille. She threw a fit of hysterics and he suddenly realised, hearing her screams, that he had conned not her, but himself. He usually enjoyed the sounds of sheer terror. He was fond of her, maybe even in love, but he was not so sure about that. He put away his knife. He told her of Queenie's plan, said that he thought Lucille too beautiful and nice-natured to kill, even for money. He did not know what to do next. He must be going soft in the head but he just could not kill her, and he would get in big trouble if he did not. Queenie could set gangs onto him in revenge.

Lucille was very upset. She did not ever want to go back to Queenie, and did not want to get Gordy into trouble. And she did not want to walk the streets, either.

'So, you'll have to work Underground,' said he. Lucille knew that this was the answer; she was dreading hearing it, though. How to get a job there, anyway? Gordy knew people, he could get her in. Then he would tell Queenie that he had killed her, and all would be well. In a manner of speaking. He would get her a job that was not too hard, watching over gauges or checking labels or something. Not everything was automated in the Underground; it had been started long ago by people who declared themselves enemies of machinery, and many of the principles they had started with still prevailed. And then, of course, there would be the question of payment to him. After all, he had saved her life.

Lucille, once she had realised that it was not money he wanted, gladly consented to settle up with him right there on the mudflats, in an excess of nervous relief at being alive, anticipation of a new life, and as a gesture of farewell to the Overworld she had always known, and out of sheer frustration and curiosity. It was not enjoyable; it seemed that he did not perhaps love her after all, or maybe he had a different idea of love to hers? Maybe her responses were dimming as the leukaemia advanced?

But what the hell did it matter?

She was given a job in the Underground in the melon gardens, and a bunk in a room with seven other people and a promise of regular meals. The melons were delicious. A strange dark grey colour, but full of nourishment. Artificial vitamins, to be exact.

There were other good things besides the fresh foods, about living Underground. For the first time in her life Lucille had found friends. Being Underground seemed to foster comradeship, and it was really nice to find that after work was done, she and her seven room-mates could share stories and little luxuries, and do favours for one another. There was no sex in her relationships although all seven of her friends were male. Mixed rooms were quite common, and some amazing orgies were said to happen, but in Lucille's commune, the best thing was the music. They were quite a good group, and she sang with them sometimes, and began to realise that Overground, living with Queenie, she had secretly been looking forward to death. Down here, she was glad to be living. Having friends was nice. They were pretty funny people though; like so many of the Underground people, they were mutants. They were really weird; if they had lived Overground they would have been stoned, for sport. Here, they led quite pleasant lives, working long hours and the remainder of the time playing music and sleeping. Nobody down here cared what you looked like so long as you could do some task regularly, although several people had remarked that she was very beautiful.

All her friends were very small, which was why there were three more than usual in their room. There was Charley, who was Mongoloid. He worked away at his simple job rhythmically and faultlessly, and did nothing but grin all day. A nicer fellow she could not wish to meet. Then there was Job, who was depressive; he was always miserable, poor man. Lucille at first spent hours trying to cheer him up, taking him onto her lap as if he were a baby and rocking him, but he always ended up weeping; he just suffered from permanent melancholia. He told her that he had been born like that, with a genetic malfunctioning of his hormones; some chemical built up in him and just would not allow him to be happy. Then there was John who could hardly keep awake. He had to be hopped up on various kinds of speed to get through the day's work, and the minute he had eaten he would fall asleep. He sometimes dropped off over his work or in the middle of speaking a sentence, or eating. That too was congenital, a form of narcolepsy. His friends covered for him when he flopped, snoring. He would have died when he was a baby if his mother had not stuck pins into him to get him to feed. In an emergency, that still worked; Lucille didn't like to do it, but as he said, she would be doing him a favour. He was very kind and pleasant when he was awake.

Then there was Alvin who gave every appearance of being slightly moronic. He was quite grotesque, with a large head and short arms, but he never did anyone any harm. The others helped him dress and bathe because he forgot how to do things sometimes. Then there was Carl, the timid and shy one who suffered from acute agoraphobia. Just the suggestion of going Overground could bring on a fit of terror so awful to watch that all the friends were very careful not to mention it. He just did not wish to meet any people other than those he was used to, and it had taken a long time for him to feel happy with Lucille around. He liked small rooms best, and finally, with her being charming, and reasoning that one more room-mate made it that much more cosy, he accepted her. And then there was Percy, who was very intelligent, and wanted to be a medical man. He had not been allowed to go to medical school because of his size and shape. His arms were much too short to drive any kind of vehicle or even perform minor operations – he was smaller than a seven-year-old child. He was ideally built for cleaning out drainage tubes on the hydroponic tanks, and he was very useful for obtaining drugs and other medicaments on the black market. He knew a lot of medical lore, some of it seemed to work. He satisfied his urge to heal people in this way. He obtained speed for John, various anti-allergens for Peter and vitamin P and B12 for Lucille because, said Percy, it would alleviate if not cure her condition. He had a hard time of it getting the right drugs for Peter because his allergies were numerous. He came out in rashes and hives, he got pains and migraines, psoriasis, asthma and heart attacks and worst of all was the sneezing. He never seemed to stop sneezing, and it was daft to call it hay fever because not only was there no hay nor had there been any in his lifetime, but his malady pestered him all the year round. Lucille took some time getting used to being sneezed upon, but she accepted it in the end because it was not his fault; he always tried to catch the sneezes in tissues, which were scarce and expensive commodities. In between orgasmic explosions and his scratching, he was a really nice person and would do a favour for anyone. So she had a good bunch of room-mates. Weird, grotesque, sick, deformed, malfunctioning, but a whole lot nicer to live with than Queenie. Sometimes she would look at Percy and dream. He was not a doctor and he was not handsome. He tried to be a doctor, and he was very kind. Still, she was lucky. Dreams and dreams was what she had, but there were not many people who even had those.

Queenie finally managed to get someone to service her Frend. For a time it functioned beautifully; it told her how lovely she was and boosted her confidence so that business was good. Then one sad day it went all wrong again. It told her that Lucille was more beautiful than she was!

She sought out Gordy Hunter, and eventually, after bringing pressures to bear on him, she found out that the machine was telling the truth. Lucille alive! He pleaded with Queenie to let Lucille alone, to spare him. The girl was Underground, she would never return. Queenie ignored him, she had forgotten his presence. She had become obsessed with the idea of Lucille's death.

'But Queenie, she's dying anyway. She can't last long . . .' She could not hear him, she was deaf with anger. Gordy left, knowing that finally Queenie had gone mad, there was nothing he could do. She was so obsessed that she had forgotten him, did not care about revenge for his betrayal. For Queenie, the big question was: How to kill that girl?

She did not want to be even accused of murder. Justice was no longer possible, and she would end up horribly, publicly punished. Something subtle. Poetic even. To get down into the Underground was no easy thing, but as a black-marketeer in disguise she might make the trip, if she bribed the right people. She immediately began making enquiries as to what was in short supply down there, what kind of thing they coveted or would find attractive. Soon she was staggering along with a valise full of odd goods, dressed as an old woman with tatty hair falling around her face. Only her vanity would allow her to believe that an old woman's get-up was the ideal disguise, but with the clothes she wore and her back bent with the weight of the valise and her face without any paint on it, she looked strange enough.

She took a lot of trouble to find Lucille without arousing suspicion. She sold dentures, underwear and hairbrushes. Finally she saw her quarry. Lucille, sitting on a high chair by some dials and faucets, softly singing to herself. Singing! Ha!

Queenie had brought a lure for Lucille. If she fell for it, she would be horribly poisoned, and nobody would know how, and if they did find out how, they would think that Lucille had committed suicide. Much depended on how gullible the girl was, but Queenie was depending on what she knew of Lucille and her naive and innocent ways. So she started her sales-talk, and she opened the valise to tempt the innocent. Lucille was instantly interested. There were few diversions during working hours.

'Oh, how lovely. Let me see.' She riffled through the junk in the valise. She did not need dentures although her teeth were not as good as they had been, but she bought a half-used rich red lipstick. The underwear did not attract her, the bits of cheap jewelry she passed over, and then she saw . . . it.

'Hey, what are you doing with this? Don't you know they aren't fit to eat?' She held up a scarlet apple, her eyes popping at its beauty, horrified because they were known to be just about lethal, full of deposits of insect spray and fallout and god knew what else. She had never had an apple to eat, they were historic fruits.

'Not that one, dearie. How long have you been down here not to know that they are developing tree-growing again? Under glass domes they are, very pretty.' Lucille was incredulous. They could grow a lot of different things Underground, but not trees, and certainly no tree fruits like this one. The colour! Everything down here was grey. Her mouth watered, but she was still suspicious.

'I haven't been down here so long, old girl. I never heard of any new apples. How much do you want for it?' Queenie then excelled herself with smooth talk. The apples were not numerous which was why they were on the black market in ones and twos. She wanted quite a lot of money for it, a rare treat like this. But, of course, if the girl didn't want to try it . . .! Lucille bought the apple and Queenie shuffled away, almost giggling aloud with glee and hatred and triumph. She wished only that she could stay to watch the results of the eating of the apple, but that would not be safe.

Lucille considered the scarlet apple. She should share it with her friends. But eight mouths around it, there would be hardly any. Even as she was telling herself not to be selfish and greedy, she had bitten into it and was savouring it. She took a second bite before she realised that it was not very nice. It was rather bitter. Doubtful, she tried a third mouthful, but by then the poisons in it had been assimilated through her mucous membranes and were doing things to her brain. Insect sprays and nerve gases and tranquillisers are very close together in atomic structure. What had happened to those insect sprays over a couple of decades was something terrible, lying in the soil, getting stronger and stronger. The nuclear fallout had done things to apples too. They absorbed very strong doses of those poisons. Lucille felt dizzy first of all, and then found that she was paralysed. She could not understand it. She had been conned, but why so violently? She blacked out, and fell to the floor, a piece of apple still between her lips.

Her room-mates were devastated to learn what had happened. They all got caught by Carl's weeping and just sat how¹ing. Percy went up to the ƒbsick-bay to see if he could do anything. They sent him away. Lucille was not dead but she was in a deep coma and would probably die soon. There was nothing to be done. She was poisoned, and because of her weakened condition due to the leukaemia, she didn't stand a chance. She would be sent to the surface in three days if she did not come around. That was the rule. Her friends were in despair.

Then the shifts changed on the medical staff and the new doctor came to look around the wards. He aimed to calculate the number of dead or hopeless to be sent up during his spell of duty, and then go and relax in his private cubicle. He found Lucille in an intensive care unit, the transparent case around her making her look like something unreal. He could not believe what he saw, she was so beautiful. Black hair, skin as white as his overall and lips as red as blood. She hardly seemed to be breathing, so he checked her record. So, this was the girl that the horrid little mutants had been pestering him about. He could see why they were so bothered about her dying. She was very beautiful. He pondered a little while, then slipped inside the tent with her. He undid the tapes of her hospital gown, stroked the hair back from her forehead. Trembling, he touched her lips. There was something in her mouth, and he hooked it out with his little finger. So, she was a suicide. How careless of the nurses not to notice. Apple was a fairly common method, but she cannot have known that to die quickly, you had to gobble the apples fast, several of them.

'Well, beautiful, you can die if that's what you want, but not before we have had some fun together.'

He went and rummaged through his drug supply and filled three syringes. Two contained a mixture of heroin and hallucinogen, and the third contained digitalis and concentrated vitamins and enzymes. He gave that and one of the hep jabs to Lucille and waited. She began to breathe visibly and a flush of colour came to her cheeks under her rouge. He hoped that she would not vomit. He gave himself a shot, fingers crossed that all would go well. He locked the door of the room.

Lucille saw the most handsome man in the world. He looked at her with love in his eyes. They kissed. Everything took on a coloured glow. He was the doctor come to save her.

There was wonderful and unearthly music somewhere in the background, almost as if it were coming from inside her own body. She had always known that falling in love would be fantastic, but this was more wonderful and beautiful than she could ever have imagined. Suns rose and trees grew against the white wall, flowers bloomed in her heart and every time he touched her it seemed that her flesh turned into jewelled universes. He lifted her up and they pranced around the room, high on a white horse. He asked her to marry him and she instantly accepted. She was in an ecstasy so great that she thought she would die.

'This is what it feels like,' she thought, 'to live happily ever after.'

Gordon's Women

Gordon had worked since the second dawn. To be monarch of a quarter of a planet requires vigilance and thought, and a sizeable bank of computers and remote-control equipment. He was a monarch of land, not people; that would be for the future, when he, as colonist, could declare the place ready for a people. Gordon had his household, which kept itself in order, and the rest was land maintenance and development. He had organised the picking of a fruit crop and purified a dam, all without leaving his rooms. He had also exterminated two surplus women, whose serial numbers indicated that they were over-aged. There was still time to fill before mid-day, the time between the two zeniths which he kept for himself.

He signalled to a woman to prepare his food, and she rose gracefully and deferentially before him, displaying a fall of golden hair on her way to fulfil his order. He surveyed the others in the room and chose the one with the plump body and light red hair, who glided towards his sleeping room when he indicated his desire. Physical boredom was sometimes a problem to him. She efficiently satisfied his needs, and sent two others in to bathe and massage him, and lay out fresh clothing. The first chosen woman brought his food, laying it before him. She smiled with hope and charm, and stood waiting to change the dishes.

Feeling relaxed and happy, he began to eat. He was not always relaxed and happy, for he had an obscure worry that he found difficult to name. He decided that in the afternoon he would visit another monarch, and perhaps talk, if there was time. It was often possible to take an afternoon off to play chess or back gammon. In truthful moments Gordon admitted to himself that his work practically ran itself, and everything else was done by the women.

Something about the food in his mouth was displeasing. He extracted a long blonde hair. The owner of the hair gazed at it horrified.

Utterly angry, Gordon strode towards his console, dragging her with him in order to read the number on the back of her hand. He punched it out, and as he did so she turned from him, but before she could even kneel she had fallen rigid, eyes closed and limbs neat. The death synapse had been activated in her head.

'Clear everything away immediately, and record I shall be elsewhere this evening. I may invent a punishment for all of you for this. I am appalled.'

When he had left, they set about cleaning and tidying, and wheeled the dead one away to the women's place. Nobody spoke. It was all and always silent. Women have never had anything to say worth hearing, and they all knew this. They were all efficient, and all extremely beautiful. Rarely did errors occur such as just lost this one her life. Three deaths in one day meant quite a lot of work. Downstairs and away, they set about all the work. Gordon must have three replacement women on duty in the morning. He must always have a hundred in his household ready to choose from for any purpose. As always, he would have his wish.

Gordon walked to the transport terminal from choice, even though it was a few hundred yards and would tire him. The suns were brilliant, and the gentle morning rain, which he had invented, had made the soil smell good. Out here where only he had ever been, he really felt like a monarch. Gordon nourished a secret atavistic longing for ancient times, a thousand years ago on Terra. Then, there had been seas and fish and mountains which men had climbed, and the soil had been worked by hand. Men must have been strong. But of course, it was just a daydream, for he knew of all the disadvantages. Violence of all kinds, diseases, and birth had been a matter of chance and good food scarce. Worst of all, male and female had lived together, in equal number, and the females, although subservient, had not had the death synapse in them, but went on living as long as men. That must have been vile and strange. But then, the history of Man was vile and strange, and long. These were civilised times, and to be atavistic was folly. He put his dream aside, and endorsed his feeling by bending to touch his warm moist soil. He had been guilty of sentiment about such things – the stuff was filthy!

He passed the rapid journey from one transport house to that in Cavin's domain in trying to name the nature of his disquiet. It was concerning the next monarch. It was time that he sired a son, for by the time a boy was grown, Gordon would be old. All monarchs must breed a successor, although none of the four on this colony had yet done so.

Cavin greeted him with pleasure, and declared the afternoon free. He set his women about making Gordon comfortable, and providing refreshments. Between them where they sat lay the pieces for chess, but Gordon was not attracted. Cavin saw, and enquired. Both men smiled, aware of how good it was to be sensitive to the other's mood, and to be so deep in friendship. It was the same with the other two men on the planet. They had often said that in societies where there were several men, friendship could be chosen, but they four had been fortunate.

'It is the question of making a successor,' Gordon put out straight away. 'It is time I got a son.'

'Hah! Your worry is death. The thought of a son might bring such a worry. But it is unreal, your time is long.'

'Not that. Not that at all. Far into the future all being well, all four of us. My thoughts are troubled on the question of which son to have. I want the best possible.'

Cavin laughed, although kindly.

'All your sons are good, excepting an accident. If you beget a defective, you destroy it, having gotten opinions from experts, you know all that. Take the medication so that you will get only males, and wait for the results. The same as for females, but for a better result.' It was not really a polite subject, but they were intimate friends. That men issued from the same source as females was embarrassing. Cavin dismissed all his women, and offered Gordon a drink himself.

'I mean . . .' Gordon persisted, drinking, 'I mean the question of which woman to choose for the mother. Surely this will make a difference to the quality of my son?' It was only the real distress on Gordon's face which held back Cavin's outright mockery.

'Gordon, you are a perfectionist in all things, it is this which causes these strange thoughts. How could the mother make any difference? Choose one you enjoy and the rest will be taken care of in the women's quarter, in nine months, Let's play a game.' Gordon declined. He was certain that it would make a difference. The closeness of flesh for nine whole months – he wondered who his own mother had been, and felt sick. But some genetic traits must be passed on from the mother. After all, they were human, in a sense.

'I do not understand you now,' said Cavin in some gloom. He suspected that his friend was going to strain the friendship with talk of metaphysics, or to speak dreamily of times long past, as he sometimes did when in drink.

'I want my son to be at least as intelligent and clever as myself. How can I know if the mother is intelligent if she has never spoken. All women are stupid and uneducated, we know – but they must have a brain *potential*!'

'You must be in a biochemical trauma, my friend. Forget all that. Obviously all the traits of intelligence are from the male, or else why are not females clever?'

'In a sense they are – they do many things after all.' Gordon was trying to distinguish between two kinds of intelligence, but even this was not what he was trying to grasp. Cavin did not look pleased. Gordon told himself he was a fool to bother at such questions, and they played a game together.

In the women's quarters of Gordon's domain, underground and a suitable distance from his own rooms, preparations were being made for the next day. As always, this included a grooming session. Hair was being washed and curled, brushed and trimmed. Every body surface was smoothed to perfection, teeth brushed; every possible physical aspect was brought to perfection. They worked untiringly, and helped one another in the way of those who are all equal. There was no question of competition for there were no special favours to be won; each stood as much or as little chance of fulfilment, life or death, as the next. They existed to serve, each an exquisite part of that crowd known as Gordon's women. Not even capable of chatter when away from him they worked in silence. Only the swish of brush on hair, the sound of polishing with scented oils or the occasional click of little metal instruments was to be heard in their hall. A gloriously formed black-haired beauty reached out to curl the eyelashes of another, while a fair creature painted her toenails in bright enamel. Dresses were chosen and cleaned, and everywhere repairs were under way.

In the nursery some attended to the young. In the kitchens preparations were made for the next day's food. Work schedules were checked, and all undertaken without a frown or a sigh.

When all was done, Gordon's women rested, recharging themselves for tomorrow's service.

Late in the night the piercing whistle announced that Gordon had sent an urgent message. It was fortunate that there were four women awake. Sadie, Heather, Judith and Mary had stayed up to celebrate Mary's birthday. To be forty years old was worth celebrating.

'Turn on a few dolls, Sadie. Gordon can't sleep.' Heather read the message. It was not what they thought, and they sat concerned. Gordon wanted an unprecedented thing, and to them it was an emergency. He wanted a 'woman' for the mother of his heir, but she must show intelligence. He had decided this might be shown by her ability to learn chess. First thing in the morning, he would begin teaching. They had never programmed a doll for such a purpose, no monarch had ever considered playing chess with one of those they all believed to be women, the android surrogates which the few real women in the underground had for decades formed to play out their impossible existence. Judith laughed, for all four of the women were experts at the game, and thought little of Gordon's ability, which they could watch as they watched all things, unknown to him. Any one of them could beat him with ease, but this was no help at all. No real woman had been in the presence of a monarch in living memory. They must programme a doll to be able to learn chess. Heather was the most clever at such electronic trickery, and was already working out a series of synapses which would cross-refer to a visual input, store all the information, and still come up with an original move from a spare bank of stored moves. She had only four hours to fix the whole thing.

'The worst of all this is that one of us is going to have to get inseminated from our store of male sperm, and produce a male child exactly nine months from the day he chooses his clever doll. He will want to see his heir growing, not like the women he thinks he sires.' Mary shook her head, not wanting that. She had found pregnancy tiring, and felt she had done her share in replacing the real humans. Her elder daughter was nine, and already an expert at replicating flesh.

'Is Gordon losing his wits, even thinking of intelligence in a woman? Could it possibly be that he might have some sympathy with our movement, if he knew of it?'

'No! He only wants to leave an heir that might be even more brilliant than he thinks himself to be!' They did not discuss Gordon or his motives again, there was work to do. This new turn of events interfered with their long-term plans, or might do so. As the daughters of the few real women of the underground, they were the carriers of a plan for a new revolution. Not, this time, a bloody one, which the women had lost, but a quiet one. They planned for a whole new world, but only when they were ready. The future was in their nursery: both girls and boys, and none with the compulsory destruct synapse, which had been the means the men had used to keep their enemies in order. There had been three generations of real people without the synapse, and no monarch had suspected that the world was other than he believed. The synapse destroyed only androids. New and ideal worlds take time to build, and Gordon and his colleagues were preparing the planet for the new free people. If he ever discovered the true state of things, everything might be lost.

'Fine birthday party I had!' said Mary bitterly.

'If Gordon knew about you, you'd have been done away with long ago.'

'Not necessarily, unless he can get help from other planets. He only knows how to kill with a number in a computer. I doubt he has the strength to kill in any old fashioned way.'

'Maybe, but all that is just talk. Let's work.' Judith was

thinking as she helped make the delicate circuits. She wondered what it must be like to get a child in the normal way. Gordon thought he knew, but sired nothings. Judith thought perhaps she would volunteer to bear the secret boy. Her own mother had known all the natural processes, but there were no grown men in their little world now, and might never be, for boys were difficult to rear – and her own real age might make a true liaison null. Sometimes Judith despaired, thinking that her own life was not even as exciting as that of an android – if those dolls experienced things, then they had more fun than . . . but that was stupid. No true woman would envy a slave. She saw her thoughts as late-at-night figments, tired and cold. She set her mind to tasks. One must be to contact all the other groups on the planet. All information must be kept circulating, they might need help with replacements. If Gordon proved hard to please in his choice of a mother, then they would be hard put to keep up the numbers. He had been known to call for a parade of all his 'women' – and he could count and check.

'Rook's pawn as an opening move? That is not intelligent,' Gordon muttered at the opening of their second game. She lowered her head, smiling stupidly. Gordon was amazed that such a beautiful little thing could learn something so complicated so quickly. He had already proved that women had brains. There was a potential which only needed using. But, of course, when he had found his choice, he would forget all that. He could be in grave trouble for heresy and political betrayal if he made too much of this discovery. The girl stole his knight on her next move. Hah! But he would not choose the first one just like that – there was always the possibility that this one was a freak.

The workshops had never been so busy, and Sadie and Heather, Judith and Mary, keeping up with the rate of destruction, began to wonder if their monarch had gone mad. They sent him dolls to play with, and he destroyed them all. Those they programmed to beat him he got angry with, and those they programmed to be careless he got bored with, and many days were passing. He was obsessed with an ideal which they could not furnish. Perhaps it was time to change their plans.

Gordon had the women set up the room for chess, as usual, in comfort, and then dismissed them all, asking them to send his partner for the day. He felt no enthusiasm for the project. He had destroyed a score of women and proved nothing to himself except that women had brain potential. His body chemistry was ripe for siring a male, and he could not choose the mother! Perhaps Cavin was right in what he had said. He had not spoken with Cavin about his present preoccupation, he felt guilt about it, as well as foolishness. And yet, what was the use of being a monarch if one could not occasionally play a game of chess with a woman, even if it was unlawful? They could all play reasonably well, in various degrees. Cavin was right, obviously it was the teacher more than the pupil which counted. Some he had paid more attention to than others.

His woman entered, waiting for the command, head down.

'Sit there. I shall first show you the simple moves, and tell you the rules.' She seemed excessively shy, this one, and sat meekly hiding behind her long dark red hair. Her dress was spectacular, green velvet with jewels sewn all over in floral patterns. He watched the light play on the jewels, and felt cheered. Her slippers were bright and pretty too. Most decorative, the whole thing. She gave off a scent he did not know the name of, a delicious and exciting fruity musk.

Gordon showed her the moves, and they played. She beat him in five moves. He was not pleased at that, as he knew he should have been – here was intelligence – but he was furious when she laughed mockingly at him.

'Quiet!' he yelled. 'I had chosen you to mother my son, and now I may destroy you!'

Judith tore off the wig and threw it into his lap, and Gordon stood up screaming like one teased with a giant spider.

She laughed at the expression on his face. She had never seen such astonishment and horror and puzzlement all at once. He was pale as clouds and trembled. Naturally. A woman with fine lines on her face, drawn by nature. A woman not perfect, and alive! And one that laughed!

He was a monarch though, and knew how to act. He reached for her hand, to find her destruct number.

'If you want to destroy me, Gordon, you will have to think of some other way. I challenge you.' They looked at each other, the ageing, thin-limbed man, and the strong middle-aged woman with the silvering hair. She was a nightmare out of his head. Or a terrible joke of Cavin's. He turned to his machinery to set in motion emergency measures, questions. It was not working.

'What are you?' he whispered, thinking into the unbelievable. 'Have I gone mad?'

'Not yet, but if you are not strong, you may be, when I tell you how the world is made now. We have decided, it is time to tell you everything, and put all things into their correct places.' She indicated that he sit down again.

'Cavin . . .' Gordon needed help.

'Cavin is with my sister. I hope they are liking one another better than you and I?' She smiled prettily, her face was almost beautiful, in the way of a man's face when it smiles.

'If we can like each other, Gordon, I may choose you as the father of my child.' She looked at his limbs. He was not strong, but that might have been because he had never really worked.

'But first, I have a story to tell you. It is a history, and begins long ago, before the revolution.' He dared to look into her eyes. Strangely, he realised that his disquiet of many weeks had gone. This monstrous creature spoke of explanations. She knew things he did not.

'We can play the pieces while I talk. I may be able to show you some moves you have never heard of. My name , by the way, is Judith.'

'Your women, Gordon. I must begin by telling you about your women.' She set out the pieces, glancing into his face to see how he was coping with the situation. Like a true monarch he was trying not to weep with rage, or so she surmised. It would take time to know if he were worth keeping. There were severe temptations. She had advantages.

Her thoughts went against the spirit of the new revolution. Gordon did not know it, but he had a death synapse inbuilt. Judith's forebears had placed it there for an extreme emergency.

'Shall you play red or white?' she asked him. Judith made up her mind. She would not destroy him. They would play a game, talk a little, and see how the new world went.

The Message

It was draughty and bleak in the hospital corridor, and Edna ached to get away, out of the place. Many of the worst scenes of her life had taken place in hospitals, and the mental scents of death, hopeless birth, pain and humiliation troubled her, turned grey the face which once may have been beautiful and filled with health. She was waiting there, illuminated by unfriendly lights, standing on the cold terrazzo, for her discharge papers to be sent down from the ward from which she had just signed herself out. She had been in Surgical for the removal of her bunions, and considered herself fit to go home. There were thick dressings on her feet inside the shoes, still a perfect fit, stretched as the old leather was by the disappeared lumps. What did they do with bunions? Burn them? Incinerated, along with the wombs, cancers, varicose veins and would-have-been babies; ashes to ashes.

It was evening, dark outside, foggy, early December. Edna wanted to get along out before the shops shut because there was nothing worth speaking of in the kitchen cupboard. She had told them that she would get a taxi, that her daughter was going to come in twice a day to see to her needs. It was a lie. She hadn't got a daughter, they could have checked that from her records if they had wanted. Dead at birth, thirty-three years ago. They hadn't seemed to notice that she'd had no visitors during the week she'd spent there. There had been two others with no visitors; both of them very old people moaning and babbling away the nights, snoring through the days, tubes, drips and curtains round both of them, all the time. Edna had put her head through the curtains when they had let her out of bed, out of curiosity. There, she had thought, even with the Grace of God, go I in a few years' time. Maybe.

A trolley came rattling down the corridor and was left near Edna as the male nurse went into the office with a folder. Edna did not look at the person on the trolley, it seemed rude to stare at someone defencelessly wrapped up in blankets. She peered instead at the notice board which told her to get her children immunised. Edna didn't believe in immunisation, natural resistance was best. But, not having had children, she was not interested anyway.

She felt her gaze dragged against her will to the person on the trolley. Great pale eyes, washed pale, set in a head made of old paper roughly scrunched like rubbish on the blinding white pillow. Grey wisps for hair, disappeared lips, drawn inwards over a whisper. Edna smiled her smile for strangers, the same smile she always smiled; a little upturn at her mouth corners, a little wrinkling around the eyes which looked away, although not this time, her gaze was held. Compelled, Edna took one step nearer, bent a little closer, to listen. It was impossible to know if this was woman or man, such secondary considerations had been cast aside with age and sickness. Edna asked: 'Are you going to the theatre then? It will soon be over with. Back in bed and recovering before you know.' She knew her words were not the right ones.

The mouth opened, dry and smooth. Like the mouth of a pet newt which Edna had nurtured as a child. Charles the newt had died and been forgotten, until now. Charles had often opened his mouth and seemed about to speak, but had never done so. Perhaps if he had, Charles would have told Edna how to look after him better so that he would have had a longer and happier life. This mouth in this ancient head emitted a sound like rustling silk.

'I wonder if you will do me a favour?'

'Of course, if I can.' Her heart sank. She did not want anyone to do favours for her, wished to do none. Not far from here was her cosy little house with its bed, electric blanket, pink-shaded lamp, its glass shade partly filled with old silk roses still as red as when they were given to her, in hospital, so long ago. She wanted to switch on that lamp, get the heating going, make some decent supper. The food in here had been inedible, soggy and disgusting. The memory of the scrambled egg would stay with her for ever as exemplary of vileness in food. Edna wanted fresh bread, fresh cheese, good coffee, maybe soup. Warmth, comfort, privacy. A proper bath without a nurse watching, her own loo with toilet paper that did not scratch. A magazine, a cigarette, all behind her own drawn curtains. Perhaps there was a letter waiting on the mat? Doing a favour for a stranger could delay this brilliant dream, could perhaps spoil it in some way. She had nurtured this dream for some days, to make bearable the lonely painful boring hours spent hunched behind a book to discourage idle chat with other patients. What favour then?

'Take a message for me,' said the head. 'I'll never take it myself.'

'A message? Where to?'

'It isn't far away, just knock on the door and give it. Please?' The eyes pleaded and commanded at once, but Edna looked down at her bandaged feet.

'I shouldn't really walk very far, I'm just going out and I had bunions removed.' The head seemed not to care about that, it was not important. The message was important.

'I've asked others but they won't. I can't post it, I haven't a stamp, and if it went through the post she wouldn't open it.' The eyes closed, reserving strength after so many painful words. But why not?

'Look, she will think it is junk mail, straight in the bin, always. I couldn't get a proper envelope.' There was scrabbling under the blanket and a hand emerged, clutching an envelope as a budgie clutches its perch. The envelope had an advertisement on it for a famous firm of rose-growers, and did indeed look fit for the bin. Edna took it from the hand which disappeared again. The voice sighed with relief.

'But where to, there's no address.' The eyes opened again.

'Number seven, just around the corner. First street past the off-licence.' Not far from where Edna herself lived, she could go that way easily. It was convenient living near the hospital, she didn't have to get a taxi, save the money.

'Well I don't know. I don't like refusing . . .'

'Well don't then. It's urgent. I'm on my way out, I am, this is my last chance. I'll die tonight.'

'Now then don't upset yourself like that, don't say such things.' Edna was embarrassed. Looking into those eyes, Edna could see that it was true, death wasn't far away.

'You will take it then?' Sheer anxiety.

'Yes, all right.' The trolley was whisked off with a squeak of rubber wheels and Edna stood holding the letter. Number seven – now which street was that? First or second past the off-licence? Edna didn't go to the off-licence, she went to another little shop. Did they mean the old off-licence or that new place? Oh God. She would have gone after the trolley to protest, ask more details, but the doors of the lift closed upon it, and she could not run. Oh God, what a nuisance.

Edna looked down at the message in her hand. Her nails had grown longer than for many years, with not having worked. She thought, perhaps I could wear nail varnish and it would look nice? But not for long, not working at Woodlawn. Her hands were always a mess. Perhaps it would be all right to deliver it tomorrow, or the day after? She toyed with the idea of a taxi straight home, about three minutes. No, it was a waste of money.

'Mrs Morgan, can you just sign this for me please? It is to say that, basically, if anything goes wrong after your going home early like this, we aren't responsible.'

'I signed that upstairs.'

'This is another one dear, that was just an application.'

Edna signed, withdrawing inwardly from the charge nurse, a young man unmistakably queer. Edna knew very well that you weren't supposed to call them that, they were gay these days, but she couldn't help it, she didn't like them, they scared her. They were always on the TV these days, dressed up like women sometimes. And they got filthy diseases. But then, said Edna's other voice, didn't everybody? Wasn't the whole world full of disease from one cause or another? Try to be fair, Edna, try not to be prejudiced. Edna sighed. Dialogues. All the time, dialogues. Swallowing first, Edna asked the young man if he knew who the person on the trolley was.

'I shouldn't discuss patients with other patients dear. Why do you want to know?'

'They asked me to deliver a message for them. They didn't say to whom and they didn't tell me their name.'

'You have a little problem there don't you? Any clues?'

'Yes, to number seven, the street after the off-licence, near here.'

'Yes. Well dear, leave it until tomorrow, you must get straight home now. Shall I ring for a taxi for you?'

'I've got one already ordered, it'll be at the front door any minute.'

'Let me carry your bag down then, I thought your daughter was coming up here to fetch you?'

'No, I told her not to bother. I can manage, there's not much in it, thanks.'

'Well go slowly, you mustn't walk far, you aren't as strong as you think, you know, you need a week at home at least before you go back to work.' Edna shuffled away, thinking, well, he's quite nice really but it gives me the creeps.

Outside, the fog was thick, condensing on the tops of cars, spreading the lamplight like bleach on wet floorcloths. Number seven. Would the street be parallel to the terrace in which her own little house stood, six streets past the off-licence? By her watch, seen with difficulty under a lamp, she had half an hour before the baker closed, but more time for the others. There was always the Indian shop, but she never went in there. Indians scared her, it was the way they looked at you, as if they accused you of starving them, although lots of them were very fat. Especially the men. Great big eyes and nothing to say, it was creepy.

Edna thought again of home and her spirits jolted up at the thought of the gas fire glowing, a radiator warming up, the bathwater heating, the soup simmering, crumpets toasting, cheese, fresh butter, coffee, a cigarette. Wonderful. To have a home of your own, a place with curtains to draw and a front door to lock, was the greatest thing in the world. Security. Safe and warm, like being in a nest. Always after work her spirits came up like this at the thought of home, especially in the winter, which she loathed. Her own home. Hard won.

Her feet felt fine although she had to walk a bit funny to avoid pressure on the joints. The baker's window was empty . . . oh, no! But she was saved, there were crumpets on the glass counter. Edna asked for three and in silence the assistant, an ugly woman with huge hands, slapped three into tissue as if she was disposing of something disgusting. Edna heard herself asking if there was someone around here, very old, in hospital, but she trailed off quickly, realising that the question was stupid, and she didn't even know what she wanted to know. Did she want to know who lived at number seven? Obvious, go and find out. Flustered, she paid for her crumpets, and the assistant, silent as a toad, gave no sign that Edna had spoken at all. Perhaps she hadn't. Sometimes she wasn't sure because people ignored her. As a child, she had been hit for mumbling and muttering, but it had made no difference. Some days, you just couldn't make yourself heard.

Walking like this, it felt as if her ankles were chained together. As if she had escaped from prison. When she was better, she meant to get herself some new shoes. Something really smart, in leather you could polish.

Her coat was inadequate. It was not a winter coat but the weather had been so mild eight days ago. Never mind, not far to go. How odd she must look, walking in this silly way. Like an old crow. Edna tried to walk normally but it would not work, something made her protect her big toes and put all the weight upon her heels. Her calves ached. It might, just, have been a good idea to spend money on a taxi after all. But to have a taxi search for a number seven, first up one street, and to wait, and then perhaps . . . it would cost a fortune. But she must not hurt her feet, perhaps she could be crippled if she walked too far? She stopped. Damn, she had walked right past the grocer's, she had been dreaming. She turned back, hobbling, determined to get a nice bit of cheese to go with the crumpets. The off-licence only had that stuff already wrapped, it wasn't any good. This was a lovely shop, one of the very few real grocers left in the town. He still weighed some things out himself on his brass scales. Edna loved to watch, as she had always loved to watch as a child, when there had been blue sugar-paper to wrap currants in, stiff red bags to put the freshly ground coffee in, and squares of greaseproof to wrap up butter, which in those days had not needed to be in a fridge like it was today. Which was odd when you thought about it, because now, things had preservative in them as well. Prunes had been dried to preserve them, and yet now, they covered them in mineral oil to keep them. Very strange how things went backwards. Here in this shop he still hung the bacon up whole, wrapped in muslin, but elsewhere it was wrapped in plastic, and went wet and rotten inside.

'Good evening Madam. May I get you something?' The warmth of that, it did you good. In the supermarket, you got a basket which pulled lots of other baskets with it, pulled a thread on your stockings, got the thing caught fast on your coat button, dropped your purse, had to fight your way past whole families with trolleys piled high, took ages to find what you wanted, walked miles up and down endless avenues, hated the music which never stopped, lost your purse again on those moving belts as you put it down to get the things out of your basket, picked it all up again at the other end and had people staring hate at you from behind because you asked for a bag for your bit of butter. Horrible business. Rather starve. The bloody music probably went on all night for ghosts to waltz up and down with trolleys laden with ghost food. Unable to find the checkout they had died in there, hundreds of them. Probably ended up as mince. Ahem ahem. The grocer, smiling.

'Yes please Mr Johnson. I'd like a bit of nice mild cheese. White Stilton if it's fresh, or the Cheshire.'

'Certainly Madam. I think the Stilton today, the Cheshire is a little bit mature for your taste.' Edna ignored the implied criticism, she knew very well that mature cheese was supposed to be the thing. But she knew what she liked.

He was already slicing a creamy wedge, only needed to glance at the scales to check that his guess as to weight was perfect, and deftly wrapped it in the paper. No plastic and sticky tape here, Edna hated it if they sealed bags with tape, you couldn't get them open without breaking the cheese. Much of the pleasure of White Stilton was gently breaking the curds apart with the tip of a knife; you hardly knew whether to watch your butter melting into the holes in the crumpets or to see how cheese broke down a natural fissure at just the correct touch, like a diamond opening. If it broke up getting it out of the bag the whole thing was ruined.

'Thank you. And a quarter of butter.'

'Danish bulk or Cornish Curl? Or Normandy unsalted?' He pointed at the palest butter, and Edna thought, yes, I'll be different tonight, yes, Normandy unsalted for a change. She wanted soup, but somehow to buy tinned soup here seemed all wrong. Silly.

'I hate to trouble you . . .' she began, cursing herself from her other side the moment she had let out the words.

'No trouble.' That was true.

'I'm looking for an address near here, a number seven. I've been in hospital and a very old person gave me a message to deliver just as I was leaving. I wondered if you knew . . .'

He stared at her with many thoughts unexpressed.

'Very old. Number seven. I used to deliver for Bowlers at number seven Carrington, and Jordans at number seven Galveston, and . . . but none of them were old. But perhaps the people to whom the message is addressed are not old? It is odd, is it not, that they did not give you more information?'

'I suppose it is, a bit.' How could she explain about how it had been, the trolley being whisked away like that, being caught out, not having time to think, really.

'Well Madam, it is not a nice night. I would leave it until tomorrow if I were you.' How to explain that it was urgent, even though she had nothing more to go on than a feeling? She shouldn't have asked, she hadn't meant to.

'I'd like a tin of condensed oxtail soup please.' The soup stood on the counter as if it had always been there, never arriving, never leaving, the things which changed were Edna and the grocer, across some unimaginable gap they leapt to where the soup waited for them in a dimension hitherto unheard of a moment in advance of now.

'You see, having been in hospital I haven't had time . . .' She trailed off. She didn't ever make her own soup, she hadn't time going out to work, she didn't eat it much anyway. She didn't have to explain herself to this man, why did she try to? She was as good as he was. Well, actually not, she didn't have a shop of her own, she had a wretchedly paid job. Ahem ahem.

'No thanks, nothing else.' On the tops of mountains, in deserts and after hospital, tinned soup was permissible for God's sake, stop looking at me like that. They exchanged words about the fog, the cold, the nights drawing in, Christmas was coming, neither of them were ready for it. Only when outside on the pavement did Edna realise that she had forgotten to buy fresh coffee. Damn and blast. Even as she turned she heard bolts drawn and saw the blind lowered on the door. She heard the man talking to someone. 'Poor old thing,' he said and then his voice was drowned by loud music. Pop music.

Coffee. No coffee. Edna did not care for tea it upset her digestion. She thought of knocking on the door and pleading but knew it would not work. The light went out in the shop.

The off-licence, one, or the other. The Indian shop. It was possible. Not far. She would persevere. Coffee was part of the picture in her mind, lovely hot fresh coffee, a real treat. That stuff in the hospital had been vile instant stuff almost all milk. Rubbish. It was all right for grocers, they could have fresh coffee any time they wanted. Edna felt hot tears starting and her other self said, 'pull yourself together you fool, stop that self pity immediately.' The tears disappeared, she swallowed, pulled her shoulders back, but this hurt her feet so she slumped again.

'Mustn't do too much on this first day out, or tomorrow, they told me, get some rest.' Well, soon, she would. But she wanted that cup of coffee more than anything, and she would have it. So there.

As she was crossing the bottom of a street going off to the right, it occurred to her that she might just as well try the number seven there. Maybe only three houses up, silly not to. Killing two birds with one stone would make up for a lot. And up this street, was there not a corner shop? There used to be, years ago, but she never walked this way either to or from work, there was no call. Corner shops were like caves, grottoes. It used to have sacks of potatoes on the floor, piles of wrapped sliced bread but not like the stuff you got now. The wrappings had been waxed paper covered in multicoloured spots of all sizes, and when Edna was little they had taken her to see the Infirmary Charity Parade, and a woman had won a prize, having made a dress out of these waxed papers. It had been a blazing hot day and they had melted and stuck to her but she got her prize all the same. Edna remembered rose petals from that day, lots of them in the dust, she had begun picking them up and got her hands smacked. Didn't know where they'd been. On the bloody flower, of course, and she'd had her head smacked too. There was very little that Edna had been able to accomplish without the price of a smack, but some of the things had been worth it. Mostly not. The judges of the Parade might have made a connection between white sliced bread slapped either side of a piece of succulent ham, and the outlined thigh and buttock of the daring winner of the contest, but in those days, nobody had heard of Freud. Nobody had really heard of Freud until most of his stuff was actually obsolete. Edna smiled, thinking, 'education, pah!' Anybody could read books and come to their own conclusions. Also in the corner shop (which should be somewhere around here) there had been a glass case with tins of zinc and castor oil cream, Aspros, Beechams pills, Compo and Bile Beans. In those days there hadn't been a National Health Service, you bought a packet of pills and carried on. And Tizer, bottles of Tizer. She never saw that now, was it still around? Her Aunt had always had a bottle of Tizer on the table to go with the beef and Yorkshire on Sundays. Edna had hated the stuff, it made her belly swell. Once, her Uncle had made a crude remark about having a baby and her Aunty, childless, had wept and hit him with the dishcloth. Those were the days.

Ahead of her she saw a light, it could be, it must be, a shop. Everything about it was wrong. There had been glass panels in the door with gold leaf lettering advertising cocoa. These had gone, the door was half open, propped by a sack of something which was not potatoes. Issuing out like a heavy gas came curry smells, the several raw smells of spices and also cooking curry, delectable and rich. Inside the shop, Edna stood and looked about her. It was sort of self service, sort of not. Paper bags hung ready to fill for yourself. Behind the counter stood a very fat Indian man in a turban, glowering right through Edna as if she wasn't there. Also behind the counter was a frail Indian girl about six years old. Her huge eyes were set so deep in her face, and her expression so sad, that had her hair not been so thick and glossy, plaited with little red ribbons and held tight with plastic combs and clips, Edna might have thought she was looking at an aged dwarf. The child looked as if she had been on the planet a thousand years, by the expression in her eyes. 'Edna,' said her other voice, 'you should be getting home now, you are very tired and beginning to imagine things.' The huge Indian stared at Edna and she stared back until the silence embarrassed her and she changed her gaze to rest on the child again.

'Please, do you keep coffee?' The girl hid her face in her hands and made a mewling noise like a kitten and the man simply stood. What could you do with people like this? It wasn't easy. Her other voice said: 'Don't be stupid, lots of shop assistants stare at you daft, in fact, most of them do these days. Not just Indians, for God's sake.'

'I want some fresh coffee please.' The man seemed to come to life.

'Down there on your right, top shelf, filter or medium ground.' Edna knew she couldn't manage to get the coffee off the shelf. Asking him to get it would be a major task. She felt like walking out. She wanted the coffee. She thought she would cry again.

'Medium ground, light roast. I wonder if you could get it for me?'

'Yes.' The little girl scurried out from behind the counter, clambered up the edges of the shelves like a monkey and got what Edna wanted. Very impressed, Edna managed a smile of thanks but got nothing from the child who went to hide again, pushing her head up inside her father's jacket and peeping out from under. Edna would never understand children, never. And a lot of other things, too. Coffee, for example did not grow in

India, they didn't drink it. Was the Indian a Hindu or a Moslem? A Sikh with a turban. What religion were Sikhs? Why didn't everybody know these things? The man really smiled now, moving his fat face about, saying something. Perhaps he was a Christian, perhaps the Jehovah's Witnesses had called, and spoken so persuasively that he had signed, in Hindi, or Urdu, some petition saying that he would not have a blood transfusion, or would support the stopping of heart transplants on the grounds of cannibalism. From purist to outright crank would not be too difficult a transition, given language difficulties and the smooth tongue of the persuader. And yet, Jehovah's Witnesses had no success with people like these. Indians must be either very ingrained with their way of life or very perceptive. Both, why not both? Edna, why do you judge everything?

'Zno verra nice day,' he said.

'No. I don't like winter.'

'Izz all?'

Edna thought. All. She was very tired, a cup of coffee would set her up. She suspected she was addicted to the stuff, caffeine. Somebody had told her to try decaffeinated coffee, but she couldn't see the point of that, you drank coffee for the lift, no point in drinking wine without the alcohol, ridiculous idea. The man picked up a can and held it out to her and she took it as if hypnotised. Okra pods. Never had those, what were they? She had read three Indian cookery books and nowhere come across these. Or perhaps she had forgotten? The coffee, just the coffee. But she wasn't communicating, because by the time she paid she had quite a pile of new things. Cardomoms, star aniseed, fresh bay leaves, chillies, mangoes and ghee. It was quite extraordinary, the way the man sold her these things. Usually they didn't try to sell you things in shops. He was still babbling and the little girl was babbling too, not in English. The ghee was clarified butter.

'You need popadams for nice curry. Crisp you see, feels different. What you curry?'

'I hadn't meant to make curry at all really, but it would have to be quick if I did it tonight.'

'Do tomorrow, get fresh chicken and soak in spices with yoghurt and lemon juice, all day, make verra good, my wife she do everything spinach with chilli everything.'

'Wonderful. Tomorrow, thank you. But I wonder can you tell me something?' He could have told her much, he could have kept her there for hours, telling her things about the world and life which, up to that day, she had never even dreamed. But she wanted to know how the numbers went in the street around the corner, number seven, was it near?

She put her purchases away in her bag, wondering what the hell she would do with them. She must be barmy, she never ever bought things which she strictly did not need. She felt her feet aching. She got out the message and turned it over, smoothed it.

'I have to deliver this and my feet are not well, I have been in the hospital.' The man took the message from her and he turned it over.

'No address,' he observed. Edna looked past him and saw some tubes stuck to a card, labelled Argabatti. Whatever was that?

'What is that?' The child tore off a tube and held it out to Edna.

'Argabatti smell nice.' Incense. She didn't want that. The Indian had opened the envelope and was reading the contents, to her horror. Edna reached out thinking, you nosy bugger give that to me, watching his face flickering with interest, side to side, his eyes going cold. He put the message back into its envelope, sealed it with spittle and handed it back.

'Number seven, not far, other side. Why you take message? Not urgent. Postman take messages, dear lady.' Not urgent.

'In the hospital, somebody asked me. It is a favour.'

'A favour. Yes, a favour.' Dawn rose over the Himalayas, and it was time to go. Edna, gathering her things together, uttered a curse on the author of the message. Not urgent. Well then, home it was. Favours, it was all very well but. What was in the envelope? The Indian knew and she did not. That was irksome, he hadn't given her the chance. Not urgent indeed, it made you angry, just after an op and all.

All the comforts and delights known as home came before her again, a gathering of emotion in the throat. Warmth, privacy. It felt like years since she had been at home, being in hospital did things to the mind, it cut you off, made you into a parcel with no fixed address, it faded your memories, wore you out.

She was going down an unfamiliar street. She hadn't checked, though. Stop. Was she walking in totally the wrong direction now? Had she turned left or right to get up this street? Was it parallel to or at an angle to her own street? Possibilities crept into her mind like woodlice, enigmatic and unwelcome. It was funny how you could live in a district almost all your life and not know some of the streets. But walking up and down streets without purpose was not the thing to do around here, never had been. Her mother had told her, don't go down there, or there, there's Irish, and roughnecks, that's slum, or, they aren't decent down there. Edna thought, nowhere is bloody decent if you had standards like my mother. I haven't been anywhere, not in my whole life, out of fear, really. But now she was here, the truth was, it wasn't up to much. Especially in this thick fog. Heathens. Her mother had called everybody but chapel folk heathens. Irish! Her mother would have stayed indoors all the time if there had been Indians and Blacks and Chinese and Iranians like there were now. There wasn't any trouble around here, only the white youths fought one another, and when had they not? Perhaps the trouble was up town, in the streets near the discos, by the big pubs. Edna wouldn't know, would you Edna? Edna has never been dancing, or drinking. Her other self was sneering at her now, it was cruel. Well, I would have if I'd had the chance. I'd like to dance like on Top of the Pops, if the truth was known, but it's a bit late *now*. It's never too late, said her other voice, never too late.

Edna felt tears again. Self pity. Of course it was too late, it was too late for everything. Women of her age hadn't much coming to them or much behind them unless they'd been lucky. Pull yourself together woman, stop that at once.

She stopped to look at the numbers on the doors, but the light was feeble, she was in between lamps. She heard a sound

humming in the telegraph wires, like the wind at dawn. But it
wasn't windy, the sound was in her ears. God woman, don't faint
now, not here. She didn't really know what she was doing, going
home or delivering a message. Both with luck, two birds. She
shuffled on towards a lamp, thinking, I am a fool to buy all these
things, they are so heavy after all, I shouldn't have been so mean
over the taxi it would have been cheaper than ghee and God
knows what that I don't need. I'm supposed to be a mature
woman, but I'm not organised even on little things.

The humming got louder as if something were zooming slowly
towards her through the fog. The houses here had a short flight
of steps up to each front door, with railings around an 'area' in
front of cellar kitchens. Most were dark, some had lights. In one
she saw a family sitting around a table, a woman standing there
with a huge pan in one hand, and she heard the sound of
television – unmistakable unnatural sound of an amplified voice
reading the news. Well, thank heavens that isn't me, I might be
lonely but I have much to be thankful for. Fancy being trapped
down there with all those children. She only just managed to get
herself up two steps and turn around to sit heavily down, grip her
bag between her feet, put her head down onto her knees before
she passed out, all except her right hand. That gripped the iron
railing as if it held the key and energy of life, she gripped as if she
knew she would die if she let go. She had gripped the rail of a
hospital bed like that, once, giving birth to the girl who hadn't
breathed, she'd put all her pain into the rail of the bed and not
made a sound herself, just felt her insides opening up like a
flower. She couldn't understand women who let themselves be
torn open, or who shouted and groaned. Edna suspected that
deep down, they didn't really want the babies which hurt them so
and were trying to keep them inside. And they used the terrible
times they had to keep their husbands in line . . . 'if it wasn't for
you' and 'how I've suffered for you'. Well, that wasn't on, that
wasn't. Her hand gripped, her feet burned. She took the pain
from her feet and passed it through herself into the railing. It
became hotter and hotter and her feet felt relieved. Let go,
Edna, just let it all go.

She spun off in black and flashes of little coloured lights into the middle of the sound, off into the hot steaming foggy nothing.

Her lips remembered a warm object, the source of all life and love and nourishment, head swimming down alone, nothing attached to it until the stomach filled with milk, mouth opened, dribbling milk and spit, luminous, sweet and acrid all at once. Swimming down, soft hands cradling, a million years ago all life was like this, the cooing musical voice, full of milk, surrounded by protective warmth. Always the sensations of pleasure swept around a central point that was slowly becoming 'I', slowly becoming. Remembering, other lives, forgetting, other loves, because here, they kept you too busy and you kept falling asleep. Rarely a shock, a pain; water too cold on the backside where backside had snuggled unaware that it needed washing, wrapped in warmth. Something hard in the gullet, back rubbed, eruption, eructation, sweet relief. The centre of the universe, the only thing in it, no guilt at being comfortable, a million years ago. The voice, like music deep and strong, invisibly on exactly the correct note.

'Dear.' Love.

'You all right, dear?' The kind enquiry. Not quite the same. She is blowing bubbles, look at her, who's a clever girl then. Look at her eyelashes aren't they long? Look at her ears, like sea shells. What a little dear she is! And where then is my father now?

'You 'ad a faint there dear.' Edna opened her eyes, fished in her pocket for a tissue to wipe spittle from her lips. The world looked terribly small, in miniature. Then she came closer in and things gradually became normal. A face was gazing into hers with an anxious concerned stare. Lillian Jagger. The strange pallor and lank hair of Lillan Jagger, a woman to whom Edna had never before spoken. Edna had gone to the same school, but even then, nobody decent spoke to Lillian. She wasn't quite all there, they had moved her to a special school, from where, along with her mother, she had gone straight onto the streets. Well known. Edna had seen Lillian with an elderly Polish gentleman in Marks and Spencers not long ago, being bought dresses.

Lillian had caught Edna's eye and then with skill like lightning managed to convey the silent words: 'He's a silly old fool but he's loaded.' Edna had tried to respond kindly without actually speaking but knew she had conveyed nothing but embarrassment. How dreadful to be bought dresses for . . .

'I think I'm all right now, thank you.' Go away Lillian, for heaven's sake go away. She was forbidden to speak to Lillian, naturally. Lillian wasn't seen out on the streets now, since the law had changed she had had a telephone put in, perhaps to replace what she had never had, the bit which was 'not all there'.

'Well you were really gone. What's the matter?'

'I've just come out of hospital, it's nothing.'

'Shall I call an ambulance?'

'Gracious no, I'm fine now.' She had almost shouted, frightened silly at the idea of having to go back to hospital.

'I'm going home. I was just trying to deliver a message first, to number seven.'

'Well it isn't far to where you live, just rest a minute and I'll walk you back if you like. Number seven what?'

'I don't know. Second street after the off-licence, I think they said.'

'Well the Ryans lived there but there's only the old man there now. What name is it?'

'I don't know. It seems ridiculous but . . .'

'You're Edna Morgan aren't you?'

'Yes Lillian, that's right.'

'I'm not on the game now you know, haven't been for years. I saved enough up and I run two catalogues. If you ever want anything you could give me a ring.'

'I will, Lillian. I will.' Well what was she doing being bought dresses for then? Had such an ugly woman a *boyfriend*? For Lillian was certainly ugly, and always had been. She had a large slack mouth which hung open, great gawpy eyes, thick legs, a protruding stomach. People had wondered what anyone could possibly see in her worth paying for, but then, what attracts men is always a mystery to women. It was a mystery unfathomable, that Lillian should not only have a house of her own, go for

139

holidays abroad, have lots of clothes and a poodle dog, when Edna had always to work and . . .

'How's the dog, Lillian?' Edna had addressed remarks and greeting to Lillian's dog, she spoke to most dogs.

Lillian's face sagged with grief, fell apart, bravely began rebuilding on the same site. Edna put her arms around Lillian and hugged her. It was not necessary to have it explained that the dog had been run over, people had predicted its death for a long time. It had run free everywhere and chased cars with frantic joy. Lillian blew her nose. Edna blew her nose.

'It's a lonely old life isn't it?' said Lillian.

'It is, it certainly is,' said Edna.

'It's coming on thicker,' Lillian said, meaning the fog.

'I must be getting home. What number is this house?' It proved to be fifteen.

'Thanks for your help, Lillian. Come and have a cup of tea some time, do.' She would live to regret this, probably. She never had people in, from a lifetime's habit, visitors were not invited or encouraged. But tonight, things felt different, she saw no reason not to have a visitor. Later, said her other self, Lillian will arrive, and you'll give her such a look she'll go right away again. You are a stuck-up bitch. I'm not, I'm frightened of people, I don't have any small talk. No practice. It was true, she hadn't had any practice. At work, she said the minimum to get by, just listened.

'I'll be off then,' and Lillian went, half turning, 'as long as you're sure . . .?'

'Thanks very much. Bye bye.' What an evening this was proving to be. Edna never had adventures, got lost, spoke to strangers, fainted. But tonight, she had. Feeling stronger, she rose and trudged off, counting the houses, thirteen, eleven, nine, seven. Might as well, seeing as she was so close.

She got herself up the four steps sidewise, one at a time, like a large baby, holding the railings. It would be a good idea to ask if they had a phone, if she could call a taxi. She had had enough, this was going too far. No bell. She banged the knocker, a laurel wreath painted black. It made a great din inside the hall but nobody answered. Edna sighed, tried again. She looked at her watch, turning it to the faint street light, but could see nothing. It was a tiny thing, a 'ladies'' watch, and no good unless you had your specs on. She listened to it, but it had stopped anyway. Hospital routine. She had never let her watch stop, not since she had been given it, a very long time ago, twenty-first present. Could it really be thirty-odd years old? Anyway, the hospital routine had put her right off her stride, it had stopped now. All your normal habits went haywire in hospital, what with the nurses coming round banging on the foot of the bed shouting 'hurry up'. Nine o'clock? No, not that late, not yet. Suddenly she said aloud, 'Aw to Hell with the bloody message' and turned to go, angry, off home, message or not, this was barmy. But bolts were being drawn, a chain rattled, the door opened, letting out light which spread like gas, yellow and poisonous.

A very small man stood there and they looked at one another, neither speaking.

'I'm looking for someone who lives at number seven, either in this street or the next. I have a message to deliver from someone in the hospital. I thought it could be for someone here . . .'

The little man opened his mouth and pointed into it, making little gobbling sounds. Edna thought he might be choking; wildly thought of patting him on the back. He pointed at his ear, made large gestures of welcome, come in, undoubtedly come in, but no words. Of course, deaf and dumb. Oh dear, she couldn't cope with this. She got out the message and held it to him, but he caught her wrist and pulled, almost toppling her. Now, it was her turn to point, at her feet and the protruding bandages, make a grimace of pain, she was good at it, Marcel Marceau wasn't the only one. He looked quite cross, this little man and then Edna twigged, she was letting in the cold.

'Sorry,' she said, and got herself into the hall, wondering, 'Do they have a phone here?' It was a cold looking hallway but vaguely familiar. The light was a bare bulb on a very long cord, hanging below her own shoulder level. Did the man have them like that so he could change the bulbs himself, being so small? It gave an eerie look to everything and blinded Edna somewhat so that she had to look at the wall, where there was a mirror in a plastic rococo frame. She looked awful. Really tired and untidy. She looked at the floor, thinking, what now?

'Look, this message, is it for here do you think?'

He waved his hands flat, cancelling, shaking his head, motioned her to follow him. The floor, of course, inlaid marble or tiles, this pattern, on her own hall at home but underneath the carpet, she hadn't seen it in years. It was nice, circles within squares, red, black and white, with a border of tiny triangles and squares. Cold though. He took the sleeve of her coat and pulled her along, into a kitchen, showed her a chair at the table, and there she fell to sitting, slumped forward, to rest. Her bag thumped on the floor so loud she thought, damn, something broken. Time passed.

When she sat up and looked, he was watching her the way people watch the dying, for signs of breathing. He nodded and gibbered and pushed a writing tablet and pencil across to her. He smiled, quite a nice smile, and banged the pad with his fist so that empty milk bottles and used pots clattered. The whole place was filthy. She thought, he lives alone, no woman. Why were men so disgusting left to themselves? So she wrote: 'A very old person in the hospital gave this message to me to deliver to number seven, a woman I think they said. Can you help?' He grabbed the pad and scribbled busily.

'I might and I might not.' Not very helpful.

'Do you know anyone who was in the hospital?'

He replied, 'Yes. You.' He laughed silently, banged the table.

Oh dear, he too was a shilling short, was nobody normal tonight? Edna felt like weeping. She wrote 'Do you have a phone?' He replied 'You've got to be joking,' and pointed at his ears and mouth, laughing hideously. Edna covered her face with her hands, exasperation, shame, fatigue, humiliation and anger filled her. He banged the table with his fist and signalled 'forget it', cancelling graphically with his hands. Edna looked an 'I'm sorry' at him and he shrugged. He went and filled the kettle and put it on the gas, then picked up her shopping bag and peered inside. He wrote: 'What are we having for supper?' Cheek!

She did not know what to do, but could not think of a way out of the situation except straight on through it. She cleared a space on the table and laid out the contents of her bag. After all, she was very hungry, it was warm in here, she was tired, why not? He seemed harmless. But who was the intended recipient of the message?

Again she held it out to him and he took it. He looked it over carefully, and propped it up in a grimy cruet, signalling with a finger: 'For later!' His eyes gleamed at the sight of the food. He began to work quickly, rooting about in his cupboards and a fridge into which she could not see from where she sat, producing cooked chicken, onions, clean plates and cutlery, chutney. He opened the ghee and soon had onions and spices frying gently, some Uncle Ben's rice boiling, the grill on ready for the popadams. Edna tried to help but he made her stay sitting down, putting in front of her a great mug of tea. This must surely be the best tea ever, it was so welcome to her she let the tears roll down, several of them and he watched them smiling. She wrote: 'Where is the bathroom, please?' He replied: 'You want a bath?' She looked exasperated and he, grinning, showed her through the back door where a downstairs toilet lurked, cold, dirty, but at least not up a flight of stairs. There was a little mirror in here, so she combed her hair and it looked no better for it. Never mind, it wasn't the Ritz, exactly.

Back at the table she watched him work standing on tiptoe to peer into the pots, dragging a little stool around with him upon which he sometimes stood to reach things, and to grill a stack of popadams. It was all coming together nicely it seemed, and then he stood on his little stool, leapt onto the table with a pan and spoon and banged the dinner-gong as they both laughed, the sound ringing through her brains like a cure. Well, whatever next?

He served up his curry, riffled through the popadams with his grimy little hands, to pick out the best ones, and these he put on her side-plate with a little bow. There was no way she could not eat them, dirty hands or not. We all eat a peck before we die, let's hope not immediately before, she thought, tucking in. It

143

was very welcome, and very good. He must have cooked many curries, it was splendid, warming her through, radiating heat and strength to get rid of the fog in her bones, her weakness, her inhibitions. Life was strange. And sometimes seemed quite good. The popadams rustled and crackled like fallen leaves, she almost said as much on the writing pad but remembered that he could never know what she meant. Soon the food was eaten, except the cheese, and this they picked bits from, she pleased to observe that he too appreciated the way cheese broke when it was carefully handled. He made good coffee in a warmed Denby jug and accepted a cigarette from her, smoking in a way which showed he was not used to it – flick flick went the ash too often.

Then he wrote to her: 'Time for bed.' Good God! But of course, he meant it was his bed-time, it was time for her to be leaving. Yes, of course, and they packed all her things away into her bag, she offered to wash the dishes but he laughed, indicating the obvious, that he didn't wash dishes until they were all used. He showed her his pot cupboard, there were dozens of plates and cups in there, it would be about two weeks before he need bother. Edna, secretly horrified, smiled and nodded approvingly, her other self said, well you know, there's a lot to be said for it, really, saves effort. Her Aunty Marion had worked like this, she'd had a curtain put up across the sink and just put dishes behind it until no more would go, and then and only then did she wash them, about every fifth day. Edna washed everything as soon as used and put it away and wiped everything gleaming. Perhaps really, after all, it didn't matter that much what way you did things, but it was *satisfying* to have everything just so, and her other self said, it's a pity if that is what satisfies you, a paltry sort of satisfaction that is. Can't you find anything better to do?

He picked up the message, almost forgot. Ah yes, he opened it, read it, looked at her closely, read it again, popped it back into the envelope, went to a drawer full of old sacks, dead biros and football coupons, found sellotape and taped it up, handed it to her. Shaking his head, no, not for me, sorry. She was halfway down his front steps, slowly getting her feet to work when she heard him say very clearly: 'It's not my message but I wish it was. Try the next street, a woman lives there.' His door slammed and she heard his locks snapping, his bolt grinding home, his chain rattling. Trickster! Thief! Cheat! He had spoken! Why would anyone pretend they were deaf and dumb if they weren't? What was going on? Taxi, she must have a taxi. No sort of good shouting for one, they didn't cruise, she'd have to ring from somewhere. Bloody hell, why had he done that? Shock went through her, anger, dismay, a feeling of foolishness. Could she knock on just any door and ask to use a phone? No, she could not. People didn't do that did they? And if knocking on doors gave you such strange adventures as a crazy man pretending he could not speak or hear, then she had had all of that she could cope with. But the fact seemed obvious now, she was lost, she really did not know which direction she was going in, and how far her own home was. It was a pickle to be in, a real jam. But there were sounds further up, somebody there, she could ask. She took a firm grasp on her bag, and shuffled forward, mouth firmly pursed against all nonsense. Well, wasn't it a simple enough matter to ask where . . .? The sound was across the street, there was a zebra-crossing. How the fog changed everything, the glowing orange, the softened sound, the great distances, the abyss beneath the feet, always, but always on the edge of an abyss. As a child, going downstairs in the dark, each step was an abyss, the last step before the longest fall in the world, she had felt with her toe, tested, every step, full of terror. She did this now, especially on the black stripes of the crossing, and her other self said: 'Edna, you are regressing, next, you'll wet your knickers.'

And there was a man, who may have called out, for now he slumped against a pillar-box, eyes closed, gurglings issuing from his mouth. Oh Lord, a drunk! And yet, perhaps he was ill, as she had been ill, and needed help. She bent towards him and got a whiff of hospital. Surgical spirit, or something like it, mixed with vomit and despair.

She was taken back twenty years. Her husband had smelt very like that one night, he had come in very drunk and gone and thrown up in the wardrobe, pissed on all her best shoes and fallen under the dressing-table. Edna had thrown a pail of cold water over him with no effect at all. She found out later, after they had parted, that his girlfriend had died after having an abortion. Even now, Edna did not know how to cope with all of that. As ever, she looked elsewhere. Her other self said something but Edna screwed herself up tight and turned away. The drunk made sounds, 'Come 'ere, come 'ere a mo', 'ere missus, 'ere.'

'What?' Had she replied? How foolish. You couldn't do anything, anything at all, with drunks. She was not frightened, just repelled. He stank, and would make no sense. No use to man nor beast, neither use nor ornament. Like you, said her other self, just like you, really. Yes, just like me, said Edna's self to her other self, yes, I agree. I work, I eat, I sleep, I watch TV, but I don't love anybody, and nobody loves me. Haven't for years. Nobody wants women of my age unless they are stuck with them; old dusty marriages that have gone on too long to break up for the knacker's yard, might as well see it through. She knew of some, the 'girls' at work revealed a lot of themselves, talking over the noise of the sewing machines. Edna did buttonholes. Millions of buttonholes. Could have been a secretary but gave it up to get married, and then look. They all had machines these days, she couldn't cope with that, electric typewriters and VDUs and whatnot. Could have been. The drunk was speaking.

'I speak to God himself, I defy him to send me to hell, I'm there. Hell is here, missus. My little girl, my wife, he took them.' He had spoken quite lucidly for a moment but now sank into his collar again, drooling. She wasn't going to get any directions from him, but it did occur to her that where there was a post box, there was often a telephone. She began to walk away, thinking, what if I drank, I'd be like that, I'd go on and on until all the pain and dreariness was soaked out of me, into oblivion, forget everything. But if a woman drank it didn't do, people left you alone, she'd seen it. Everything was different for women. Everything.

"ere missus, missus just a mo . . .'

'I can't, I have to get to a telephone, I'm not well.'

'I'm sorry to hear you say so, very sorry. If you've got your health, you've got everything.' He subsided again, this time into immediate bubbling snores. Got everything with your health, have you? Well, she hadn't found it so, she'd been healthy and had nothing. Empty.

Degenerates were more to be pitied than despised, but what could she do? Take him home and give him a bath, feed him? She'd never get rid of him, it was a ludicrous fantasy. But something ached to nourish and nurse, to do something good. She wasn't any good, not to man nor beast. Tears began to roll.

'Pull yourself together, you old fool.' All right, I will. And she swallowed so hard it hurt her throat, blinking at a fuzzy lamplight which broke up into shafts of brilliance through the salt water standing on the brink of her vision, obscuring everything but their own dazzling beauty. Moons and stars and lamps, all these and firelight Edna had viewed through dazzling water-broken rays. There were footsteps behind her. She could not hurry. Hope, just hope they would go on by. It was the drunk, he grabbed her arm, swaying about.

'Let go, go away,' her voice said, rising thin with fear.

'I'm not going to hurt you, I only want, want, I only want to, I only . . .' he seemed to have forgotten what he was saying, he looked upwards as if something hovered over him. Edna pulled her coat but he had a firm grip on it.

'There's a telephone somewhere.' He was trying to help.

'Yes, let go.' She was frightened but had calculated that with one swipe of her bag she could knock him off balance. He let go of her sleeve only to grip her wrist so hard she yelped, heard a thin scream rising out of her.

'Don't be frightened missus, nothing to fear from me . . .' and he went into a series of horrible coughing laughs at his own words, 'Nothing to fear fro me-e-e-he-he-heh', until Edna heard her thin screams turn into hysterical thin laughs, she giggled stupidly, it was like a tussle in a school playground half serious.

'Gi'us a kiss before ye go then?' and he lunged at her with his

147

wet stinking mouth.

'Off, off, get off, away . . .' She was surprised at her own strength, surprised that she didn't faint. She had always thought she would faint if a man attacked her in the street, it would be so frightening she would be paralysed. But she didn't spend much time fearing attack, she always stayed in at night. It was a long time since she had been out after dark, she had not realised that what she read in the papers was really true, here, in her own district. She swung her handbag and made a solid connection with the side of his head, his grip loosened and he fell like a tree, slowly but surely, to Mother Earth. Edna had shuffled herself to the intersection of the streets before she began trembling. Oh God, please God, let me get home, *please*. Men, how disgusting they all were. She had little to do with them nowadays but whenever she did, it was only to confirm her worst suspicions that they were all, to a man, quite disgusting. Thought only of themselves, never occurred to them that it might be an utterly ghastly experience to be the subject of their attentions, their desires, their needs. Always theirs. Give. Give me. Never, never ever, how can I please you. Hatred and loathing flooded her and the trembling stopped, her breathing eased. Anger. If her feet hadn't been bad she'd have *kicked* him too.

And now, standing at the intersection, her feet began to impress themselves on her consciousness. They burned and throbbed. Fear of damaging them brought tears again. Dammit, what a stupid thing to have happen how *stupid*. Please help me, please, I'm lost. I'm lost!

This must be the worst night of my life. She got out her hanky and blew her nose. Worst. But it wasn't. She remembered very clearly which that had been. The night her mother had died. Lying in the big double bed that Edna had once been thrashed for creeping into, to snuggle into the warm smells. Her mother's thin face on her narrow head had cut back deep into the pillows like a hatchet, looking very threatening amongst the lace trim, her thin wisps of hair dry like steel wool, her feet under a cage to keep the weight off them. She had had pints of fluid drained away from her legs, and out of her belly where Edna had begun her life, but more seemed to appear from nowhere, she never drank much but swelled up all the same, the lymph gone crazy. Weak heart. Edna had thought, yes, use it or lose it, not a lot of love gone through that heart, it hasn't any muscles to speak of. Life in the eyes, two dark beads sunk in the skull, flickered spasmodically. Edna would always remember the looks of disgust in them as her mother looked into Edna's eyes. Hatred even. Words issuing from her gummy slit of mouth though, trying to mollify, to deny the look in the eyes.

'Edna I tried to love you, I wanted to. I loved your brother the best, I couldn't help it, I wanted a boy.' No mention that night of the ruined leg that had been the fault of Edna arriving in a clinic where they had puerperal fever, so that Edna's mother always had ugliness on her as well as the unwanted burden of a girl. The leg had been lumpy and much bigger than the other one, with purple veins threading it which always made Edna think of potted meat from the butcher's – his vile brawn which had bits of bone hidden. Hatred. Awful, awful hatred, from her mother, and returned in full measure.

The eyes had begged forgiveness. And Edna had reminded her mother of what she had so often said.

'But you said to me that you would make me wish I had never been born.'

'Just an expression Edna, that's all.'

'You succeeded, with your expression.' Muttering 'horrible old bitch' Edna had pushed past the nurse at the door and stormed down to the kitchen to make cocoa.

And then stopped in the act of making cocoa, brushing tears from the back of her hand, burning little splashes as hot as milk, glittering evidence of distress magnifying the beginnings of brown age spots on the veined, hardworked hands.

'She never showed me how to love.' It was not a typical thing for Edna to have said but it came from somewhere deep in her, standing against the scrubbed wooden table with the clean newspaper near the cooker to catch flying grease-spots. It came then and it came now: She never taught me how to love. She hadn't known how to love, how could she teach the art? The poor woman, oh God, the poor woman, how could I have turned my back upon her. How could I? Because I had learned from her how to be bitter, she taught that art well. Pride inherited prevented.

Taking a delicately sugared Nice from the tin, she recalled now the grittiness of it between her teeth as she had thought, this is our last chance. I can make it up, I can go and take her in my arms and say 'there, there, I know, I know, nothing is your fault, it is all right, you are my mother, we never made a go of it but it is all right now'. Rinsing the spoon beneath the tap, drying it, putting it away.

'I'll go up again.' In a little while.

Took the cocoa, stirred the fire in the front room, turned on the television and watched an interview between an Indian guru with long hair and a perpetual smile, and a hard-looking man representing the Church. The guru talked a lot about love. Carnations flooded the studio and the man from the Church smiled as if he was scared, not at all liking joy and religion so blatantly mixed. Edna didn't care for it much either, the guru's hair looked greasy although it was probably oil; to be fair, his white gown was immaculate. Love cures all ills does it?

When she went upstairs again the nurse was tucking bits of cotton-wool into orifices, a bowl of disinfected water nearby, the eyelids were closed and the doctor rung for to make out the certificate. Not one more word did Edna speak until after the funeral when she said 'Have a slice of seedcake, Emily' to someone who had come a hundred miles with a black eye-veil, and in her heart had said 'Have a slice of the body'.

Remorse is a terribly painful feeling, and it can go on such a very long time. A lifetime, even. But was it remorse, or just plain guilt? What was the difference? It was important, to know the difference.

Edna in the cold fog could not decide which way to go and felt so very tired. She went and sat herself down on the steps of the nearest house, thinking, perhaps they *won't* mind if I ask to use the phone, or ask directions. But if someone knocked on her door at night she wouldn't answer it for anything. The fog was freezing onto the pavements in a beautiful glitter, she couldn't sit here long. She could feel the cold striking up, she would get piles, pneumonia.

'That's what you get for doing good turns for people,' she moaned, fingering the message in her pocket, and worse, the good turn hadn't got done yet. She felt as if her toes were on fire, splitting apart, but knew that really this could not be, wasn't scar-tissue stronger than skin? She'd heard that. She'd been told to get a taxi home and she hadn't, out of meanness. Served her right. Yes, serves you right, you skinflint, said her other self scornfully, but, what are you going to do now? Look at you, instead of being safe and warm at home, tucked up in bed, you are freezing and exhausted and lost. You thought you'd walk to save the cash. Walk! After an operation on your feet! Now Edna, doesn't that seem really *crazy*!

She thought she heard music. Well, for sure it was not a heavenly choir, but Black music, very loud now as a group of youths rounded the corner, one of them bearing aloft a huge stereo transistor like Atlas holding up the Music of the Spheres? Edna looked at this giant and he looked at her, she was surrounded by them, four well-built lads, two with long locks. She thought, something is happening to my mind tonight. Can it be the anaesthetic still? I'm not frightened and I think like I used to think when I was at school and wrote poetry. For two pins I could write some more, I could put down thoughts and get all sorts of new ideas like pictures in my mind, connected to things they had told her at school, Greek Myths, Babylon, Egypt, Palestine, eunuchs and pashas and dancing girls, harems and vomitoria, great feastings and swords thrust into pomegranates. Burnished swords, yes, she still didn't know if burnished meant polished or burnt in the fire to a dark colour. Polished would look better. What did they use – they never had Brasso then?

'Missus, you'll get the cold sitting out.'

'Lady tink dis Jamaica!' They laughed. They were not threatening. She couldn't think why they'd stopped though.

'You waitin' someone?' Edna shook her head. 'No, I'm lost, I need to get home, I was trying to deliver a message, my feet

151

hurt, been in hospital, very tired, don't usually sit on steps at all.'

'She mean she lost man, lost in de fog tonight, man, that's bad, where you live den?' Edna told them. 'Well, that's a way up dere, you lost de track all right, you need a taxi.'

'I couldn't find a phone box, I was looking for a number seven house too, near the hospital, I was taking a message but I haven't found it yet.'

'Seven? Seven, you say. Dat de odder end de street man, some ways.' Tears suddenly spilled out, oh dear.

'Hey man don't cry, it not far.'

'Man look at her she bushed, she feet killin' her.'

'Well Missus we home now, livin' here.'

'Ask her in, make a brew.'

'Yeah, Alice make a brew, can't leave her out here.'

'Lotta white women leave us out on de street all right.'

'Aw shaddup Dobie, what you want de revolution to*night*!' They laughed again, real laughs and strode up the steps past her. One of them took her bag and gave her a lift under her arm.

'I should really be getting home you know . . .'

'Sure you should but you ain't gointa make it widdout some tea and a warm, and Dobie here will go and ring for a cab, won't you Dobie?'

'Hey man it has to be me?' They all got inside and the light on and the door closed and somebody shouted down the stairs, 'Hey you lot, turn that bleeding blaster down, this ghetto is trying to sleep!' The giant complied. Edna thought, this is really strange, the music sounds better loud, I never liked loud music before except a brass band. A door opened and a pale-faced girl peeped out, long hair in myriad red plaits all with beads at the end. Pasty but pleasant, she smiled.

'Hello, what's happening?'

'Make some tea, Alice, dis woman dyin' in de cold sittin' on the stoop and she lost herself.'

'Oh. Right.' Alice smiled at Edna and beckoned her to follow, and Edna, holding onto the banisters and the wall, managed to get herself along the passage, down two steps and finally accept a seat on a sofa, in what seemed to be a kind of dining kitchen.

152

The girl began making tea and got out some packets of biscuits. She did everything very slowly and calmly. Her clothes were a challenge to Edna's charity. A shoddy old cotton skirt that would have disgraced the Oxfam shop, a washed-out cardigan with a hole in one elbow, some thick red stockings with socks worn over them inside some huge embroidered slippers, ear-rings in profusion and, appearing above the neckline of a tee-shirt which had been hacked across with scissors, a tattoo of roses between the girl's breasts. There were tattoos on her wrists as well. The gas fire was on, and on the rug lay a number of cats in a heap; black, black and white, white, tabby, and then, to Edna's delight, made out three kittens nuzzling in. Edna got out her cigarettes and offered one to Alice.

'Where were you looking for?' asked Alice. Edna told her the address, apologising for how silly she was, she knew it wasn't far away and she'd lived here for years, she couldn't understand it, really.

'I expect you got yourself into one of our circles, I'm sorry about that. We've been practising circles and if you get inside them and we don't take the power out, you can't get out.'

'I don't think I follow.'

'No. Well, I'm into magic at the moment, and if you make a circle of power around the house you can draw into it those people you want to come, but sometimes other people wander in and then they get lost. Don't worry, I'll turn it off and somebody will get you a cab. Here, have some tea, do you take sugar?' It was all said in the same tone of voice, as if tea and magic circles were all about as important.

'Not as a rule, thanks.'

'There's no milk, I only get it for the cats and it isn't perfectly fresh I'm afraid. Anyway, this is Jasmine tea and it's better without milk.'

'Oh thank you,' said Edna, beginning to sip the scalding brew which had a pleasant scent to it. The girl was probably a shilling short, tonight was the night for that kind of thing. But she was very nicely brought up, there was something about her that told Edna she hadn't always lived like this. Now, she looked like a dropout – but they didn't have those now. Now, it was just people on the dole. Pushed out. On the wall was a very strange poster of a sort of Indian woman with dozens of arms holding dozens of faces and more arms holding different things, including skulls. It was so intricate and full of things happening that it made Edna dizzy to look at it, so she looked at the cats. But she wanted to look again and Alice said: 'Have you seen pictures like this before?' Well now, that was a strange question, because perhaps she had but goodness knows where it might have been. At home she had a picture of a country cottage by a stream, with a little bridge and a man standing there fishing. That was her sort of picture, but this one was fascinating.

'I can't say really, I seem to have, but I don't think so.' She looked around her and saw other posters, the sort of thing you sometimes saw in shops, pop-stars and whatnot, with painted faces. It was a strange world, when you thought. Painted like savages, Edna had always thought, and yet, there was one which she couldn't deny was attractive.

'You've probably seen it in another life. Have a biscuit.'

'Thanks, I think I will although I've not long since eaten, strange to say. I got invited into a strange man's house and we cooked a curry.'

'Oh that's nice, who was it?'

'Well, he was very small and he played at deaf and dumb but when I left he spoke. I don't know what to make of it really.'

The girl seemed to take it as normal that a man would play at deaf and dumb, and then suddenly speak. She thought a moment, ah yes, 'That would be Mickey, he lives round the back. He's a bit loopy but he's very nice. He's quite harmless. He plays the guitar as well.'

'As well as what?' asked Edna, drinking tea, peeping over her huge cup with the violets on it at the cats, at Alice, and at the poster of the many-headed woman.

'That poster is Kali, she's a major Indian goddess. As well as selling newspapers, he stands on the corner by the Post Office.' Oh goodness, yes. Of course she'd seen him. And heard him, he had an extremely loud voice which carried a very long way. The old scoundrel; she'd been had on and right! Alice put the cigarette she had accepted from Edna on the little mantelpiece over the gas fire, and turned to Edna with a serious expression on her young pale face.

'How did you manage to get lost so near to home? I've just noticed, the cats had spoiled my magic circle so it couldn't have been that. Naughty cats!' She stroked them and they responded as a heap. Edna saw for the first time that in the hearth there were several sticks and bunches of herbs and a small stoppered glass bottle. The sticks had been in a star pattern but it was broken. Edna felt embarrassed for the girl in some way she could not define, perhaps she should have felt fear, but this was too silly.

'Lost? Well, I was on my way home from the hospital. I've been in there several days to have bunions off my toes, and as I don't live far from here I thought I'd save the taxi fare and walk. It seems insane now when I think of it, but that's what I did. But there's more to it than that. You see, I was given a message to deliver by a very old person who said they would die tonight, and as it was almost on my way home I thought I would do that. And it was foggy, and I got confused, and now it is getting late and I'm very tired and I haven't delivered the message or anything. Have you a phone?' But no, they hadn't, one of the lads had been going to a phone for her. Where had they gone?

'Where was the message to? I might know them, I know most people around here.' Edna got the message from her pocket and told the girl, number seven, but she didn't know the name. 'You see, they were whisked off on a trolley before I could get any more information.' Alice held her hand out for the letter and did not even look at it, but held it to her forehead, eyes closed. After about a minute she spoke.

'It's a bit confused, but I could probably get it clearer if you like. But you'll have to promise not to tell anyone anything you see or hear in this house. You seem all right to me but some people aren't to be trusted with secrets.'

'Oh I am, really, I wouldn't tell anything, whatever can you mean though?' Edna was slightly offended, tell secrets, indeed, but what secret could that be? The girl called out, Robert, Robert, have you got any skins, and very soon two of the Black youths came into the room and sprawled themselves about. One of them handed Alice a pack of cigarette papers.

'I'm going to do a psych on this message, this lady needs to know where it should go and even maybe what is in it.'

'Alice you crazy, she straight.'

'It's all right. She can keep a secret, she has promised.' The young man shrugged and flashed a glance at Edna who smiled nervously.

'Make more tea, Robert, there's a good boy,' Alice told him, and she was splitting open the cigarette and re-rolling it in three papers stuck together, scraping into it some little bits of brown stuff. Oh God, thought Edna, this must be that drug, that marijuana. Oh God, what now? She thought, Black men, drugs, rape, madness, oh God, please help me.

'Excuse me but I think I'd better be going,' she said in a wavering voice, trying to get up but it didn't work, her legs went from under her. She was utterly fatigued.

'It's okay, we'll get you a cab, don't be frightened. I said I would do a psych for you. Sometimes I need this to get opened, don't worry, it's cool.' Cool? This was like some play on television, people didn't say things like that in real life.

'Yeah man, she cool. Have some tea.' He refilled Edna's cup and she, stunned into silence, thanked him with a nod and a nervous little smile. Alice smoked her new cigarette for a while then passed it to the silent youth, who smoked it and passed it to Robert, who smoked it and passsed it to Edna.

'No thanks, I don't think so.' Without a word he passed it back to Alice who smoked it and passed it on again. She held the envelope to her forehead, closed her eyes, and the only sound was a purring of cats and the faint sound of the gas fire. Oh God, please let it be cool, thought Edna. The smoke smelled very pleasant, and she lit another one of her own, offering the packet without speaking, to shaken heads also in silence.

'This message is to a woman, very old, who is just staying at number seven until tonight, then she will go and not be found.

The message is three words only, I can only see the word 'forget' because it is folded in paper with a lot of words and figures on it and pictures of roses. It is an urgent message. The person who sent it is a man and he is dead but still nearby, he is anxious that the message may not reach its destination and be understood. There's nothing else.' She sighed deeply and gave the message back to Edna, who was very impressed in spite of herself. 'Forget'? Whatever could the other two words be?

'Well I think I'll take a cab to the address and then home, I don't care about the money now, I just want to get it done and get to bed, really.' Robert passed her the cigarette and before she knew it she had taken a deep drag. She stared at the cigarette in disbelief.

'Good God, look what I've done!'

'Don't worry man, it's cool.' Alice took it from her smiling. 'It's harmless, don't worry. I'll tell Dobie to get the cab.'

'You can't, Dobie's gone out again, there's a blues.'

'A blues, I didn't know, where?'

'Ambrose, him a blues, they got in the sound.'

'Might go, what do you think?'

'Give it a little time, it's early yet. I'll phone. Hey, where you live den?' But Edna had gone to sleep. Her one and only tiny drag of dope had relaxed her, and her body had said, right, that's enough, good night.

Did Edna dream, that night? Ever afterwards she could not say what was dream and what was real, quite. She dreamed, if she dreamed, music and dancing, roses, cats, and a glorious circle of white light which kept floating through space towards her and then receding with a singing humming sound. The white light was very beautiful and made Edna feel rested and loved and good. She dreamed that she was tucked in under blankets, that cats slept all over her warm and purring, and that during the night a lot of people came into the room and stood around looking at her, whispering, and then went away again. She dreamed that she spoke to her husband, saying, I understand really, now I do, it's all right, it was just life, I couldn't take it and I didn't know how to love, I don't blame you really; and he

157

replied, well, I loved you the most but I got tangled up with Barbara and then all that happened, a man needs some comfort but we never made a go of it, did we, and I'm sorry, please forgive me Edna, and Edna felt, yes, I forgive, of course, it is all past and gone.

When she woke it was to tea and toast and people laughing and fooling and loud music throbbing away and she hardly knew where she was at first.

'It's still very early,' said Alice. 'We've only just got back from the blues and we'll be going to bed soon, have some breakfast and we'll get you a cab.'

'The fog's going, she could walk. It isn't far. Dobie says her address is just around the corner.'

'But she must take the message.'

'Yes, where do I take it, oh dear,' and Edna began to feel wrought and sad again.

'Please, Alice, can I use your bathroom?' And while she was in there she thought, well, I feel a great deal better for that lovely sleep, I really do.' Her feet didn't hurt any more, she felt almost perky.

Back in the kitchen the Black youths were dancing a strange dance with their eyes closed. Edna watched, fascinated, and then pulled herself together.

'I'm going now, I'll walk, I've decided. I must thank you all very much for helping me, I'm truly grateful. And any time you are passing, do drop in and see me, won't you?' Only Alice replied, 'Thank you, I will.' The young men were in a world of their own with the music.

So there she was out on the pavement shortly after dawn, the daylight dead-looking, a corpse of a day which would not rise easily. From inside the house she heard William Blake's hymn, 'Bring me my bow of burning gold, bring me my arrows of desire . . .' but no, it was not being sung, it was loud music, the tune, 'Jerusalem'. Not like she had heard it before, done differently, like those rock groups on the television – she usually switched them off. This was thrilling. She stood listening, and softly sang along. Inside the house, Alice took off all her clothes, and began a witch dance to the music of Emerson, Lake and Palmer, rearranged her sticks in the hearth, joint smouldering, eyes cool in the distance where they looked, seeking and finding.

Well then, which way? Left, to the top of the street, seven should not be very far away, this was ninety-three and she began a slow countdown: ninety-one, eighty-nine, eighty-seven. And then the music seemed to begin again, rhythmic, clashing, bells on the cold air. The sound was familiar. It was a milk-cart, indentified by the low humming behind the rhythmic clashing, and the thin whistle of a milkman who was clearly enjoying his job. Well, if a milkman couldn't help her find her two elusive destinations, nobody could.

A few inches at a time her feet overtook one another and she looked down at them encouragingly, not far to go now, feet, we can rest in a hot bath, make some coffee, put you up on the sofa by the fire and all will be well. Television on, or the radio and some knitting, everything normal. Back at work in a week, until then we can just enjoy ourselves in our own way. And then, oh bloody hell, she was looking down, not at her own black leather low-heeled court shoes with the bunion lumps worn into them, but a pair of large Oriental embroidered slippers, with a five-pointed star on each vamp, in blue beads, little flowers and patterns stitched in pink and yellow wools, a silk tassel in blue dazzling on the toe of each. How? Well, she had woken up without shoes and put her shoes on, how stupid. Oh dear, she would have to go *back*. She couldn't be seen anywhere in things like these, although truth to tell they were very comfortable, and really attractive. You could wear things like this in the privacy of your own home, perhaps. She visualised herself at home in Oriental slippers, a dressing-gown in silk with a dragon on the back, perhaps, her hair stylishly held up with a large comb with a butterfly on it, she would spray scent on herself in the mornings, and not get dressed until lunchtime, answer the phone over coffee to the many calls of friends, some of them men. A whole new Edna. And have interesting things on the walls, a stereo so she could listen to her own choice of music, have people to supper once in a while, go out, even, to the pictures or a pub, or to a Chinese restaurant for a meal, with a man, and talk. She saw herself dressed smartly during the afternoons, a valued secretary, or, better, having her own business. She could sew, she could set herself up in business, design the dresses herself and charge a lot because they were unique designs. She could finish details better than most of those she ever saw in shops. Perhaps there was a market for this kind of thing, still? She saw herself getting on a plane and going for a holiday somewhere wonderful, not just Spain or France, but the Far East; she would be adventurous and see things for herself that most people only saw on television, she would get new ideas for dresses, buy interesting silks and scarves and tassels and things in Thailand or China or Burma, she would return loaded with beads and coloured fabric and then make wonderful clothes, and she would perhaps have a shop of her own. Her things would appear in magazines on beautiful young women, and it wouldn't matter that she herself was getting on, she would be recognised as clever and original. Sewing button-holes could go to hell, she would have a factory of her own. She would have her own labels, it would say Edna Originals, and people would want clothes with her label neatly hand sewn into them.

'Morning Mrs Morgan, you are out early today!' It was her own milkman.

'Yes, and also, I'm lost. It's the fog.'

'Yes, it's been bad but it's clearing.' It hung around like chiffon shrouds and at the end of the street Edna saw a pale glow which could be the sun. Her slippers stayed still now, they would not move, with their patterns, like Qeeqeeg, they had decided to die. Her ankles were puffy in their thirty denier tights in beige, horrible things, she used to have more style when she was younger. When she got better she would go in for coloured stockings, there was nothing to stop her going in for some workouts, a gymnasium, get toned up again. It could be fun. And swimming, she hadn't swum for years, at one time she could do half a mile easily. The bottles had stopped rattling like marbles in a bag – they had called them glass alleys when she was little, she had had dozens of them, the feel and sound of them was still very real. Some had been milk white with streaks of twisted blood in them, very beautiful. Her hands now felt small, as they had as a child, those hands which had struggled with an inky pen at school, always stained with ink, the hands which had scratched her head under the tight curling-rags at night, loosening a tight hair here and there to make life tolerable, and the hands which had picked her nose, pale green fascination, irresistible picking for which those hands had been smacked, dirty girl! Those hands had had three tiny warts between the fingers of the left hand, and the nails had been difficult to keep clean. Scrubbed more than once a day, poked at with a nail-file, her hands had curled up like terrified hedgehogs beneath the edge of the tablecloth for fear her mother would see their intractible grubbiness. The palms sweated and would taste of salt, should she delicately touch one with the tip of her tongue, smell hot in summer of bluebells and grass and soot and bright sickly sweets. They had once not been strong enough to turn the taps off properly, big brass taps over the sink, they had hurt her fingers. When they had become strong enough to turn off the taps so that nobody else in the house could turn them on again, Edna had felt very satisfied. Green marks on the taps, *verdigris*, the drip from the tap into the stone sink, splash splash like tears, but cold, cold like the mornings with linoleum under the feet. Where have I been going that I have arrived here?

'Mrs Morgan, are you all right?'

'Yes,' she whispered, smiling into the pale sun. She could not speak properly, her head felt too heavy, there was no room to open her mouth, move her tongue. Her cheeks felt huge and had no feeling in them, she had ceased to feel cold, it was very pleasant really. She tried to think of what to say, to ask about the number seven, smiled to while away the time until she got it all sorted out in her mind. everything was of equal importance, standing here, going there, getting home, not getting home. She was about to take a totally new direction in life, everything was going to be a lot different and a lot better, she knew it for certain. It was getting it started, that was the first step and just now she couldn't move. Her thoughts ran slow and cold, the cream froze into crystals some mornings, there on the icy pavement milk ran, brilliant diamonds splitting slowly and the voice of the milkman saying, blast and damn, oh bugger it now I've cut myself, and red streaks running in the white glass very beautiful. He was kicking it all now, into the gutter he scraped and cursed and spoiled the pattern, somebody will hurt themselves on that if I leave it there, oh dear, do pardon my language, Mrs Morgan, look luv, are you all right, what's the matter, Mrs Morgan?

A ginger cat came to lap at the milk which was left, she could hear its rough tongue scraping.

'It's an ill wind, Mrs Morgan.' That blows nobody any good. She had never understood that as a child, she had thought that ill winds always blew bad, she had been slow. The cat thought it a good wind, it was enjoying the creamy milk, pussy pussy, nice pussy. Intent, it lapped.

The milkman was offering her a lift on his cart, she began to take a step forward but it didn't work. The cat looked up at her and their eyes met.

They exchanged a long look of pure love.

The cat went away. Edna closed her eyes at last. There was a high note of pure sustained singing, very beautiful, it spiralled upwards lifting her spirits with it, above the fog, over and over in a pearly void. She was poised up there for a long while, floating in a happiness far beyond happiness, she was bigger than herself, she was spread out vast like a cloud of golden light, singing the note, up and up, unfolding more until she was a giantess filling the sky of the world.

But then she began to return, slowly, lower down, floating down, becoming small again, sliding back into her waiting body, it felt tight and painful, oh, sadness, oh, it had been lovely out there, and when she opened her eyes finally, realising that her mouth was twitching with an ecstatic smile and that her breath was moaning with the bliss of it all, there were people around her, and she was in a bath of warm water, a nurse massaged her limbs efficiently. She remembered this nurse, she was very kind.

Hospital again. They dried her and wrapped her in a gown,

put her on a trolley, put a drip into her arm tucked her in with many blankets, and she was wheeled away.

'You'll be okay in a few days, Mrs Morgan, don't worry. You were very naughty signing yourself out. You need more rest.'

The trolley stopped outside the office. There was a tired-looking woman standing outside the waiting-room looking impatiently around her. Edna gazed hard at the woman and eventually their eyes met, the woman's face pretended a little smile.

Edna spoke, the sound emerging like a whisper.

'My coat, in the pocket, please.'

'In here, you want me to get something?'

'Yes.' From Edna's bundle of things eventually the woman got Edna's coat, and then, the message.

'Can you take it for me please? It's urgent. Number seven, second street past the off-licence, near here.'

'Well, can't it be posted?'

'It's urgent. Please.' The woman looked trapped, cross.

'Well, all right then, I suppose. Yes, of course.'

The orderly returned and wheeled Edna away down the corridor and into the lift.

The message. Forget. Three words said Alice. Forgive and forget. Forget-me-not. Lest we forget. What was it, and who was it for? The woman would take it, it would get there in time, that was the main thing, wasn't it? Edna smiled happily as the doors closed and they began to ascend.

Heads Africa, Tails America

In Africa the clouds never cross the sun. Clouds countable, racing, dispersing and gathering, fill the skies of Africa and yet they never veil the sun. That I read once and believe and the idea attracts me violently. Perpetual sun. Cosmic cosmetic glamourising protective layer on my greyish hide, sunglasses and bright lipstick, beautiful at a glance. For what enhances the human frame more than colour? Deeper than bronze I would bake, for even in England I have achieved miracles of transformation in two days on a withering lawn. And in seven days become bleached beneath the clouds that do most frequently obscure the sun.

Yes.

Now when I was in a bar in Greenwich Village, sitting shivering in the heat of a New York August, this because I was wet to the skin with the waters of Washington Square fountains – the temptation to douse myself publicly and thoroughly having proved too sudden and great an onslaught on my sexual mores (and what else would have prompted a woman to wet herself to the skin whilst several hundred hippies in various states of degradation watched and whilst her male companion looked on unmoved except for a faint startlement appearing in his otherwise controlled pale blue eyes) – shivering all the more violently because not only was the bar too efficiently air-conditioned so that even the sweat of normal people in the bar dried before it had properly beaded beneath the arm but also the man I was listening to spoke of Africa. He did not tell me that the sun never hides behind the clouds, he did not mention the weather at all, but mostly the beautiful scenery in East Africa, most particularly Kenya. I manifested as one born under blazing sun. In any other climate such people shiver. Some poor wretches arrive in England with the sun in their blood and never feel warm again. Though I have not touched the tropics in my feeble wanderings, I felt that I had the sun in my blood. I thought: how could my blood congeal with benison continuous?

Outside my window now, in England, the skies are clear, the sun is yellow on the white garden rocks, and birds and butter-flies are active. Second flowerings occur. Almost November.

Exquisite, excellent, and, in case the nights prove cool, the house is centrally heated. Yet my marrow is solid and my breath steams and icicles, crystallises on the rim of a cup. I sweat rime, I do not bathe but crack open my shell and step out of the shattered fragments, clean, cold. I wept last night and rhinestones woke me, embedded in my spine, my own tears taken shape, sharp. And my hair . . . oh that . . . it is like the winter lawn cuttings – did you know that to cut the lawn with the hoar frost on it is good for the grass? Snap and tinkle goes my brush and little fragments that I must remember to look at under a microscope fall conspicuously onto my black-clad shoulders. And my teeth, how they ache at contact with water, how the brush scratches and brazes down into the soft nerve with burning cold, how I could scream into the blue handbasin if only I did not fear I should strike the right note and crash it into splinters. And I am menstruating rubies and bloodstones and pink opals. At first I thought it was sacramental wine it was so thin and clear and mean but it froze solid and lost its odour in the mineral world. So I have to take care of my fingernails and drum up a little warm breath now and again to soften them lest they break away. It is getting harder and harder to breathe warm, it is getting harder and harder to breathe at all.

Africa, you would thaw me out I know. And yet I fear to live in you, your men are far too tempting and I can *always* resist temptation nowadays. I have learned strength and the consistency of moral fibre and the value of faithfulness, but not without enormous pain. I am a great one for suffering. People have been known to despise me for it, and also, but less often, love me because of that capacity.

It was nice to hear David talk of East Africa.

'Farms of white set in trees, each more perfect than the one before. It was too much for me.'

'Was it David?' I said. And I further enquired how it could be that he lived in squalid New York when the best places in the world were obtainable to him. He had hitchhiked around the entire world, why not go again?

Oh he had to live in New York to keep his head straight.

'I see.' And thought that Africa would straighten my head, that it would, and true. Not having at that moment thought about the frustration of seeing a thousand ideal lovers every time one went out to buy a bit of cheese. It would be too much, one's head would not only grow askew, it would burst, ripe with substances more appropriate to other body parts. Thoughts of Africa and of a rather dull party I attended in New York, perhaps the only dull hours I spent there. I am reminded of an African ballet we all went to see many years ago in the North of England. The dancers had blue-painted nipples and excited my senses more than anything had for months. Afterwards in the pub I fell to dreaming of fancy-dress parties in my studio, everyone wearing raffia and blue poster-paint, dancing wildly until Sunday dawn. Aloud I said: 'We'll definitely have to have an African party.' The place was silenced until they comprehended.

'I thought you said "a fuckin' party" for a moment.'

Perhaps I did. Are not such floating fragments on the sea of the unconscious called Freudian ships?

'Oh David, tell me about it,' I said, shuddering so hard I could not hold my glass. 'Did you go to the Mountains of the Moon?'

'Yes I did, of course I did, and the Great Rift Valley.' And he told me of high craters set about with giant weeds and, sitting numerous on the ground, dappled panthers, naked and slithery in the moonlight; plateaux unexplored and the metallic light that would not keep the head straight.

Oh Jesus Christ I could have wept into my beer.

'You are shivering,' said Tom who is an observant fellow, he being a professional writer.

'Yes, I was watching my limbs shaking, it is interesting, I cannot think why I shake quite so much, I am perfectly relaxed.'

He left the bar to go and purchase a second-hand chair which later proved too large to go into his apartment without removing the door which might in turn ruin the doorbell connection. I thought of him lonely and unvisited, sitting in his apartment in the chair, wondering if the chair had been a jinx on all his friendships. The fact of him having a telephone spoiled that joke

. . . oh surely they would call him on the phone? But if *all* one's means of communication fail, do people come and tell you about it?

It is nice to arrive at a destination and discover that it is the one place on the planet that will keep the head straight. I found that New York was that very destination to me once I had taken a few deep breaths and looked around. I loved it and, strangely, it loved me back. I felt blessed walking the streets, I felt warm and alive and I could find my tongue, it was like being reborn, I had an answer for everyone and I also had things to say from myself. Whoever *that* was.

There was a hippopotamus in a pond on a cold day, and we approached it eagerly and stood amazed as it explained to us about itself. Our children were entranced that a hippo could talk. Its voice was very deep and very slow and it opened its mouth with apparent difficulty, slowly and muddily enunciating its likes and dislikes, the name of its natural habitat (Africa) and a warning about its powerful jaws which were capable of breaking a man into two pieces, although it seldom did so. Oh, hippo from Africa, are you not cold to the bone in that English slime? Where is your mate? When do you mate? How often? Do you wallow in your cool distress and groan and grunt for a suitable mate, do you sublimate your sexual energies by eating salted peanuts thrown by the crowd, producing instead of orgasms enormous stinking farts? Do you long for the sun to bake a crust of mud onto you, do you wish you could jump into the fountains of Washington Square on a hot summer afternoon and get wet through whilst the Americans watched? A hippopotamus in the fountains, what a gas, natural gas, it smells suspiciously like sublimation, exhibitionism. No, no it is just the hot weather, anyone with the sense would do it, I am now so cool in the breeze it is a delight to be alive. To add to our comforts, let's have a beer in a bar.

'You are shivering,' said Tom who is observant.

'Y-y-yes,' I said and made no further rejoinder although I am observant too, I have swivelling eyes that stand up above the water. David was cold also, he had followed me into the fountains, but either he had not got so extremely wet as I or Africa still warmed his blood. Both.

The sun has gone, great banks of late October cloud obscure him, a wind whips up the rose petals and lawn trimmings. If I go outside, I will get motes of dust in my eyes and that will spoil the shine of the ice. Refrigerated amber beads with dust on them, could anything be more sad?

Had I whole strings of such beads I would wear them around my neck and go and live in a corner of Washington Square, and watch the hippos splash. Or I would trade them with the tribes of East Africa, tell them of the magic properties of frozen human eyes, make with the eyes at the lovely inhabitants of my mind and bare my sparse bosom to the burning sun.

As winter approaches I think more and more of hibernation. I store salted peanuts under the rather hard mattress and I have cunningly replaced the stuffing of one of my pillows with little cubes of nourishing vitaminized fudge more normally used to take away the appetites of fat people. I stay in bed later every morning and go to bed earlier every night. I am Ursa, the female bear, and I am not pregnant with cub either. I shall not have to wake in January to give birth or anything sordid like that. It is very pleasant to curl the paws around the ears and draw up the haunches, hear the prairie winds like a mistral fade into the distance with its popping of corks and murmur of friendly waiters and flap of white linen and oh such lively talk. Big Bear pulls on cowboy boots and crunches over New York snows, twenty below and a girl in every taxi. He never went to Africa, he went to Paris and caught dysentery, came to England huge and shivering and used our bathroom facilities about thirty-nine times although I was not counting, just marvelling that anyone could be so brought down and yet have such verbal energy, and worrying also in case we should run out of toilet paper before he departed depleted. Oh Ursus but I could have comforted you by snuggling into your massive back just where it aches and taking over the task of stroking your moustaches for a while, so that you could sweat in peace in that brightly coloured nursery room where we put to sleep, and put out the light in your eyes, and I would have shared my store of peanuts with you; we could have stayed there all winter and slept all through our dormant sexuality, snuffling our way to the bathroom at increasingly infrequent intervals and I could have offered you a square of the vitamin fudge, growling: This removes the appetite and keeps the head straight.

Snuffle snuffle growl pad.

'Mummy, there's a bear in my bed.'

'Good heavens, dear, are you sure? Come with mummy and we shall frighten him away.'

Great Ursus, named Marc, left us a bottle of pink champagne. We had meant to drink it all together but what with the dysentery and his desire for ice water, and what with Colin's ulcer trouble I wasn't going to drink it all myself, was I? It lay in the fridge until Saturday when we opened it and gave some to the children who sneezed and giggled and went straight off into strange dreams and Colin swore it didn't affect him at all and I felt instantly drunk.

My head was far from straight. I wept into the bubbles and said some horrible things and went to bed by myself and curled up, first checking on the winter food supplies and that was when my temperature started to drop even lower. Hence the sharp pangs of rhinestones and the banging about in the night when Colin came to bed.

'Someone's been eating peanuts in bed.'

'Don't be silly, I never touch them, you know nuts give me the wind.'

Well maybe we are going to go and live in Africa. Yes, we'll definitely have to have an African safari.

'Bearer, have you got my portable bath, my portable handbasin and portable toilet?'

'Yassuh mam.'

'Have you got my portable Washington Square fountains, my portable food blender and my portable central heating system?'

'Yassuh mam.'

'Have you got my portable television set, my portable lawnmower and my portable double bed?'

'Yassuh mam.'

'Jesus Christ, you must be so tired. Put down the bed and get into it alongside me.'

'Mam, you know you got rhinestones in your bed?'

'Yes, I'm saving them for the winter.'

'You should meet my cousin, he works down in Kimberley.'

'Goodness gracious me, how loudly these tribesmen snore!'

It will be cool this evening so I shall light a fire. But such a dangerous occupation for one so deeply frozen, what if part of me thaws, I shall drip onto the carpet and besides, I should not be so active with my low blood pressure, I might damage my brain cells and then: My head will not be straight.

At a party in New York there was a lady who had written a book on how to grow avocado pips. I have an avocado plant eight feet tall as it happens so I had no use for her book but I noticed now apt it was when some gallant commented on her appearance.

'Like a young Karen Blixen.'

'Oh she wrote so exquisitely about Africa,' said both David and Tom in the air-conditioned bar, and outside in the New York sun they spoke of her writings and I said I had admired her too but it had been many years before. I could visualise the coffee plantations in flower and knew that I wanted to travel to Africa, and, God help me, write about it afterwards.

Well, I got the fire lighted, the coals caught up and reflections of hot light glimmer in my brass and copper, could anything be more English? We had trouble with the fire the night Marc stayed, he was very interested in the small flame I managed to induce from the bucketful of nutty slack. (Damn the coalman for delaying delivery.) Marc knelt down and peered into the tiny fire as if he might see his future there, I recalled an uncle on a hearthrug long ago growling for me to ride on the bear.

'Again, uncle bear, again, let's do it again.'

'Not just now dear, I seem to have caught the dysentery.'

And like all well-trained good little girls I did not cry and howl selfishly, throw myself on the rug in a tantrum or bite his leg but went into the kitchen and chipped off some crystals of ice that had formed around my eyes, dropped them into a glass tumbler and decorated it with a slice of fresh lemon and returned with it to Marc who thought that he would never see a glass of ice water in England. Oh but it is a country of marvels that Americans would never expect.

The conversation just then was about Tarzan and the myth of the free wildman and all that crap. I said to Colin:

'Well why are you so damned keen on living in Africa and swinging in trees in municipal parks whenever you get the chance if you aren't still sold on Tarzan?' I was sorry I'd said it the moment I realised I had said it, I had hurt his dreams of Africa. But not half so much as he will hurt mine.

And my temperature is going down still, everything is getting slower and slightly distorted, time had less and less influence on me, only yesterday I had the dinner ready at four in the afternoon being under the misapprehension that it was well after six and time the children were fed.

'But mummy we've only just had lunch.'

'Have you dear, I didn't notice, I was asleep in bed.'

Marc is asleep in bed when Tom rings him in the middle of the night. By a certain tone of voice Marc can tell that he is in for a long conversation. I wonder what kind of a problem it is that could keep Tom talking for an hour or more in the middle of the night? If I lived in New York, would he call me up with his problems? It does not seem too likely, all the signs indicate that Tom and I will never have a really intimate friendship, the pass key to that requires something more than mere admiration of his work and a personal attraction, and whatever it is, I do not think that I have it. One thing I do have of Tom's is an old cap. But maybe the things he discusses with Marc are not so much personal problems. Maybe he wants advice on how to get a second-hand double bed into his apartment, he has been obliged to sleep downstairs in the vestibule these last two nights, it won't even go into the lift. If someone rings him in the middle of the night he cannot hear the phone.

'Are you out of bed right now?' asks Marc sleepily.

'Yes, I was too hot to sleep tonight anyway so I stayed in my apartment with a lot of friends.'

'Have they any ideas on how to get the bed into the apartment?'

'I daren't ask them, I'm not intimate enough with them to approach the question of beds in apartments.' Together they laugh at the joke. It is like when Tom and I saw two old black men in the Bowery fighting desperately with their crutches. Tom just about broke up laughing, a strange, high, utterly delighted and slightly diabolical laugh. I felt very polite and silly in my amusement by comparison, which goes to show that one must never compare oneself with writers like Tom, especially as one hardly knows who they are, you have to be careful with whom you mix – psychosis is more contagious than German measles and can also cause a woman to give birth to some unfortunate monsters. I know how easily caught are curses and psychoses; I can remove such things from people by begging an article of their clothing and wearing it in public. I have a cupboard full of old clothes and a closet full of succubi in alcohol and people tell me that I am uncommunicative these days. They ask me why I have had the phone taken out. To save expense and interruption, I reply. Interruption? Yes, I'm hibernating.

Who said Tom was psychotic, I didn't, I only said he might be, anyone might be, these days you never know what you are talking to, do you? Just because he did not invite you to dinner, will not discuss things with you, does not exert himself to make your weird little existence more fabulous whenever he gets the opportunity?

The truth is I'm as jealous as hell of his magnificent tattoos and his capacity to ride a powerful motorbike. I can't ride a motorbike, I have tried, but I fall off. Too unstable you see. It's going round bends that's dangerous, and you also have to know your way back.

'Do you think I would like it in Africa?' asks David who is Tom's friend from way back, no he didn't ask me that, nobody asked me that, they don't care whether I would or not, it doesn't affect them at all. But Marc had a dream of Mombasa once, and that seemed like a sparkling coincidence if ever there was one. As a student of Jung I am interested in synchronicity, being unable to explain certain series of coincidences. I turned to Jung as always, for he is the Philosopher for the Next Hundred Years, and I do not like to be left behind. It was a hell of a coincidence that Marc was visiting England and I lived there. It could be nothing but synchronicity at work that Marc was going to Paris and so was I. It could be nothing but a complete balls-up on Jung's part that my trip was cancelled and Marc went traipsing around the *Bois de* something-or-other taking photographs of American exiles who used the slang of fifteen years ago.

It must be synchronicity that I live here and now, have just lit a fire of coals in preparation for a cosy evening and am about to cook a tea of sausages and eggs and bacon, it being Monday and no cold meat in the fridge. A friend came yesterday and stayed for dinner even though it was the middle of the afternoon – 'Well if it really is only four then you have time to stay,' I said, and between us we ate all the roast lamb except for some scraps which Colin made into sandwiches. I hate making sandwiches, the fillings always elude the bread.

I cannot keep my bread straight.

I lay in bed the night before last and I started to swell. I gradually expanded until I filled all the bed and Colin began to moan and snore in his sleep and I heaved to accommodate my newly enormous body, and he would have fallen onto the floor except the covers must have been well tucked in. My tongue got enormous, it grew at first at a greater rate than my mouth so I had to open my jaws. Back and back they creaked and grew slowly big enough and squared-off at the front, my top lip and my nose became all one huge mound of flesh. I knew that if I sneezed I would blast the bedcovers right off. My great stumpy arms and legs rested heavily across my vast belly and my little fat ears twitched. My insides began to rumble like a distant volcano. I was almost too heavy to move and everything was incredibly awkward, but somehow I managed to get a hoof under the mattress and scoop out some of the salted peanuts. Most of them rolled onto the floor but I managed to throw a few into my gaping maw onto the domed tongue and slowly close my lips over them before they rolled into my throat. I chomped noisily, slurp slurp, in the otherwise silent night. I thought of creeping downstairs and opening a bottle of champagne but I knew that champagne is meant to be shared amongst friends and I was the only hippopotamus for miles around. I called Tom, long distance to New York at a cost of several pounds per minute.

'Tom?'

'Hullo. Who's that?'

'This is Josephine. Tom, can you help me, I have a problem?'

'A problem – you've got a problem?' He laughs delightedly, I am pleased to have made contact so easily, perhaps he is telepathic?

'Yes, listen. I can't get through the door to the toilet and I think I have dysentery.' I listen to his wonderful trilling amusement until I reckon I have spent about enough to get me a bigger bathroom built and ring off feeling better already. I make the whole room tremble with a wonderful bassoon-like stale-peanut-smelling fart which reaches an impossible vibrating nadir and then rises to a crescendo like a Swannee whistle and dies away on a series of staccato squeaks and a final flabby silent gust. I am small again, about a hundred and eight pounds – most of that ossified brain cell. I turn over in bed and Colin struggles for air dreaming of Africa. In his sleep he speaks. 'Jesus Christ, how these native women snore!'

Yes, it had to be synchronicity that made me small again by the time my little girl called out in the night.

'Mummy, mummy, the curtains are coming out at me!'

I stagger quickly into her room and growl at the curtains.

'Back back you rose-patterned poltroons, back I tell you! How dare you frighten my little girl?' She is already asleep, secure in the knowledge that I can deal with anything supernatural. With curtains like ours how could I ever leave her behind, who else has the power to subdue them when they try to attack in the night? A child needs a nice stable mother in this crazy world, someone to reassure her and help to keep her head straight.

So I shan't be setting off with a rucksack to the wilds of Greenwich Village alone just yet, and if we get to Africa it will be as a family, because in Africa there will not only be a plethora of curses and witches and bogies and so on, there will be snakes and spiders under the pillow (things I can't deal with but Colin can – you should see him hunt with a slipper –) and elephants on the road and crocodiles in the only decent swimming water for miles. I shall be needed to warn and nag and exorcise. We shall go on weekend trips to the Mountains of the Moon and see the shimmering leopards from the safety of our Land Rover, and see the Blixen-type coffee farms and see hippos in their habitat. If we went to America we should go to look at bears I expect. Family trips are like that. In Africa I shall get a magnificent tan and seek out African writers and ask them questions and with luck they might even ask me questions too. I might even write an African novel!

Excuse me, the telephone is ringing.

'Hello, who's that?'

'This is Marc in New York.'

'Oh, how lovely to hear from you, how are you, are you quite better?'

'Oh yes, lots and lots better thank you, Josephine, I've been eating avocadoes and they seem to have an – er - curative effect you know?'

'Oh yes indeed, I'm sure, I have one eight feet tall in my sitting-room.'

'You do? I never noticed it! But listen Josephine, I – er – seem to have a problem.'

'You've got a problem?' I can hardly stop laughing, I know it is costing him several dollars a minute but my laughter is not to be contained by such a consideration. I can dimly make out what he is saying over my noisy mirth.

His bed is full of rhinestones, he can't understand it, he cleared them all up only the other night and took them out and gave them away to Chinese people on the street. But here, the bed is full of the damn things again, they are terribly sharp and they are ruining his hibernation.

'Send me your red scarf, I'll hex them for you,' I say, but the distance between us seems to spoil our usual instant understanding. I cannot seem to communicate properly. And besides I am laughing so much. It is very amusing to be called like this in the middle of the night, especially as we haven't got a phone.

The Pollyanna Enzyme

It was a great party. It was one of the best parties that any of them had ever been to, and they were saying so. Everybody in the buildings was down in the community centre which had hardly been used since the place went up, and they were drinking, dancing, flirting, fooling around. Somebody had brought out some balloons and streamers 'to make it like a kind of a New Year's Eve Celebration' and everybody thought that that was a good idea and very funny. All the children were tearing around making a great racket but nobody minded. Let them do what they wanted – why not? Somebody had an antique flag collection, every nation there has ever been, and they brought these to the party. The funniest thing, which made everybody happy, was when Major MacBrayne helped the guy put them up, dangling them out of the window, draping them, enemies together. He said: what was the point of nationalism, this was All Nations, it was fine by him. They made a good display of colour.

There was unlimited drink and smoke and anything else required to make a party go, for everything had been free for a week in all the stores. There had been no looting or rushing – just a steady shopping without all that waiting at the checkout. The food was better than usual, they had been lucky with what was available. There was plenty in the warehouses, nobody worried. So everybody was pretty high on goodies, but they were high anyway. The party was into its third day. There were some marvellous scenes to witness. It was marvellous, for example, to see Mr Emechta from the fourteenth floor actually kissing Mrs Partridge from the fifteenth. They had been enemies for years, the police had had to be called at times to separate their fights. Mr Emechta always said that she was noisy and that he couldn't get on with his embroidery and his meditation for her doing goddamn ballet exercises day and night. They had fought, thrown things, sued, cursed. And now they were kissing. They would surely be making love soon – would it be in his place with its North African mats and beaded wall-hangings, or hers with its *barre* and mirror and not much else? They both lived alone, having brought up and launched their families years before.

There were tears as well, of course, but all good parties have at least one weeper. It was a mean looking man from the third floor, a Joe Sainsbury who never bothered much with anyone but had always kept himself to himself. He was a painter who did arid abstract things to suit his nature, and who had refused point blank to look in on Mrs Gleason, the very fat one, when she had her stroke. He was the nearest to her who didn't go out to work, it wouldn't have hurt him but he had refused. It was now hitting his conscience and he was sitting next to Fan, who grinned at everyone with her strange new crooked smile, holding her podgy mitt and weeping, trying to get her to forgive him. She kept on saying that there was nothing to forgive, she was sure she would have done the same, he mustn't worry because it was bad for the digestion. But he was enjoying his remorse too much to knock it off quite yet and she was enjoying the attention, so what did a few tears matter? A teenage girl took them a bottle and a plate of pies, which was unlike her as she was Alley Sally, the leader of a Ripup gang. The gang seemed to have disbanded.

There was a crashing of glass and a strangled cry from the opposite corner and people stood back and other people crowded near. 'Give him air!' went up the cry, but there was a reply: 'He won't know what to do with it – he's dead!' and everybody laughed themselves silly for a while, and were almost too helpless to get him stretched out on a bed across the hall. They pulled the covers right over him and told one another not to forget to call the doctor, or whoever.

'He was looking forward to it – he's missed it. ' That too was funny.

'Well actually, he hasn't missed it, he just got it sooner than expected.'

'Poor man, he always was in too much of a hurry, a real heart-attack temperament, never could relax.' Well, he was relaxed now – until *rigor mortis*.

Out in the hall all the telephone boxes were full. Lots of people felt constrained to call up relatives they hadn't spoken to in years.

'Well I've been meaning to come and see you, really I have,

but you know how it is and the time passes, how are you anyway?' That was Doctor Goldman from the lower floor – 'Come to think of it,' said one of the guys who had moved the corpse, 'I think we left it on his bed.' They tried to tell him about it but he was engrossed in his conversation, they could see over his shoulder that he was conversing with an old person. Very old.

'Well I'm not too good really, Samuel, no I'm not too good. I have twenty-three pieces of spare part now and, to be honest, it's not the same as your own stuff. It all has to be maintained and the repairs are expensive and have you ever tried putting on your shoes when your left hand is at repair and the one they lend you doesn't fit your brain? I mean, I've been thinking life isn't worth living. But now I'm content.' All those years at prosthetics college and his Mama was still prejudiced against spare parts. She had never trusted his ideas.

'Well I'm certainly glad to hear that, Mama, and if I can find the time, I'll come up for a couple of days – no, I'll promise now. Will that be nice?'

'Nah, forget it. There's no point in clinging on to clapped-out relationships. You may as well enjoy yourself now. Who wants to visit a heap of old metal and plastic anyhow? Your real Mama went in the incinerator years ago. I still love my little boy, isn't that enough? I should be hugging him to my artificial heart.'

'Mama, you were always too generous.'

'That's right, but who's counting?'

They were standing in line, but nobody was pushing, they all knew they would have enough time, nothing was that urgent. If they didn't get through, why then it was a good enough reason for not getting in touch. Did it matter so much? There would be forgiveness, with a bit of luck. There was a good excuse for everything now, it was a privilege to be alive at this time. Everybody felt that, as if they were special people all of a sudden. After all, nobody else had ever been in on the End of the World before. It had uniqueness, as a situation in which to live.

Out in the plaza a pupil of Jean Partridge danced an original dance to 'Not Having to Keep Her Dentist's Appointment'.

Besides being a brilliant dancer, she was also a dental phobic; fear beset her in pathological amounts at the mere mention of drill or probe. Fortunately for her she was in no pain so she was free from her one great worry. Any other kind of prosthetics did not worry her but life still held the horror for many of such a simple thing as the fitting of a crown. She was in luck; she need never visit a dentist again. She did a couple of cartwheels. It was wonderful what freedom from fear can do to the muscles and creative flow. Soon, others joined in her dance for reasons of their own. The plaza was full of joyous movement.

'It reminds me of the wonderful spirit we had in the antiray bubbles during the last war.' This, of course, was Major MacBrayne, who had loved everybody during the last war because he had been having such a good time. It was too late for anyone to point out that his attitude to 'people' from outer space, who were still not allowed immigration permits and were only communicated with by media, was quite atavistic as well as stupid. He was what he was – retired . . . at least he was harmless.

'They shouldn't be called people, it's not right, anybody with tentacles is not goddamn human and that's that.' He was often coming out with such remarks but as he was getting old and had probably left it a bit late to get himself a new brain, nobody minded. It was just an opinion, and at least you weren't getting shot at for this nowadays. His companion agreed with him. It was Sophie Barnstormer, the social worker, the girl with the prosthetic head. She suddenly seemed to have no work to do because so many of her problem clients had disappeared with this new development.

'Yes, Major, I agree, it's wonderful. There was a terrific spirit of comradeship, and all petty differences were put aside, and what's more everyone was a lot more healthy. It was the simpler diet and the draining away of neurosis into planned aggression. It's good for you!'

'Precisely put, dear girl, exactly so. Such good old days, they'll never come back again.' This pearl of irrefutable logic struck Sophie right between the eyes, almost dislodging a circuit concerning polite response.

'Yes, but this is even better,' she managed.

Pearl Weldon, the hospital assistant was the last to give up work. She was drinking her way steadily through a litre of Ouzo but would calm down in a day or so. The thought struck her that it was better not to be blotto at such an important time. She had been working very hard for four weeks on the testing. Everbody had been to a clinic six times for various tests. The penalty for not going to a clinic was death, and it had been very effective because at the time of the testing, the news had not yet leaked that there was not to be much life left for anyone, if the immunity factor could not be found. If even one person could be found to have immunity, then it might be possible to create a suitable anti-toxin. Meanwhile, Staff Nurse Weldon was gloriously drunk, smiling out of the window at the pink evening clouds.

'Ain't never goin' to that clinic no more. Finished with that is what I am. No more blood and urine for me – Ouzo from now on!'

There was no immunity factor against an enzyme – it was presumed to be an enzyme because it most resembled known enzymes in behaviour – which has not even touched human flesh before. All living cells were affected. The heat of the outside of a space module had not destroyed it, for that was where it was presumed to have come from, although it was also theorised that it simply came in on a kind of dust comet, a self-propelled vortex which dispersed itself upon the airs of earth. It laughed at all radiations and all known chemicals, viruses and other enzymes. All it liked and all it did was to lodge in a living cell's nucleus – and it was yet impossible to see in what manner it penetrated the cell wall – and there cannibalise the energy for itself. But it seemed to do nothing with this energy except burn itself out, ejecting all the electrolytes and making death inevitable. Both for its host and itself. It was therefore an unreasonable creature, ruining its own environment – but good sense is after all a human concept, and even if it has been observed to pertain to everything humans know, this is not to say that it pertains everywhere in the universe. Where this thing came from, there was no reason or sense, or evolution, for it was suicidal not self-advancing; it was an existentialist enzyme, it seemed to be about to destroy all life on earth just for the sake of doing so.

And yet not even for that, for there is after all no such thing as a 'sake' – either if you get lost in the deeps of linguistics or if you are an enzyme from elsewhere. No 'sake' was going to start or stop it from wiping out the whole of life on earth within approximately two more weeks. Everything and everybody would go at about the same time. It did not require contact to spread, it seemed to have come in gusts on a wind, first an occurrence in the Australian desert, and then, but not yet completed, world-wide coverage. One tribe, one of those hundreds occupying Australia after the last of the whites had been driven out, had died overnight. It was this that had given the first warning of what was to come. It was thought that it would take a total of nine weeks to kill, and some heroic labs were still busy testing plants and animals but few really hoped to find an answer at this stage. Testing also was an existentialist occupation for they knew it was useless and yet they were committed. Each to their own.

The question of human behaviour in the face of the inevitable was most interesting, but even that was not widely discussed after a while. Everyone was suddenly very civilised and pleasant and kind; this was the result of the inevitable, the feeling of being in the same boat as the rest of the world. But some mind which delighted in academic exercise for its own sake averred that the new behaviour was a direct result of the enzyme upon brain chemistry, a metabolic miracle. Maybe it was a combination of both factors. People who did not waste their brain power on such futile questions were beginning to call it the Pollyanna Enzyme, for obvious reasons.

Many people set about fulfilling lifelong ambitions while there was still time. Some ambitions were grandiose and some were reasonable, but nobody minded that other people did as they pleased any more.

It got back to the buildings that one of their crowd had

achieved his ambition in a manner of speaking. Charlie had always wanted to climb the Himalayas. Now was his chance . He had been married for twenty-one years, and he told his partner and almost ruined her death. She had imagined them holding hands, making love, being together. But if he wanted to go off up a mountain at a time like this he wasn't the man for her after all, was he? It was no good holding him back, it would ruin the scene. She decided to make the most of her own life in her own way. She told him what her intentions were and he had to accept the inevitable. He hadn't realised that she had been discontented. He was sorry.

During his preparation time they were almost as affectionate as they had been twenty years ago. One of the reasons for this astonishing renaissance was that there was no future. It had been the future which made her cry in the night, heartbroken and facing her death without the love she craved. Now, that seemed irrelevant: love on the short term anyone can manage. She was sure that once he was off up the mountain, the mountain which had been used as an imaginary refuge from her attentions so many times before, she could find what she needed. All the terminology had changed. She no longer had inhibitions about words like 'casual' and 'extra-marital'. Well and good.

Charlie, travelling light, managed to get a plane, and then a train, a mule, and finally a long walk. He imagined that he would be king of the world up there, in touch with a god he believed in, nearer to everything pure and clean, up there in the cold and the beauty, elevated, alone.

There was standing room only, it was a very common dream. Many people had the grace to laugh, turn back, secure in the knowledge that they were not the only ones cheated of perfect solitude. Charlie decided that he too had a sense of humour and tried to laugh. It broke something that hadn't been used in years so he jumped off a precipice. Others followed suit.

The woman back at the buildings, if she knew, did not waste time in mourning but poured her pent-up love on whoever wanted it, and there were many to choose from.

Some of those would-be mountaineers did not kill themselves

but stayed on swapping mountain stories and, once the ice was broken, finding that other people are not hell. They were all talking about themselves and so hardly noticed that nobody was listening, but the spirit was there. Nobody gave as a reason for climbing a mountain that old cop-out 'because it was there', there is a reason for everything and they struggled to tell the truth. The High Peak became a massive psychiatrist's couch.

In the buildings such questions were no longer a worry. Life was okay and they were together more than formerly. They worked out a rota for cooking and cleaning so everybody had more spare time, and they wished they had done it years before. Other things that they wished they had done years before, they did if possible. One old lady of much more than one hundred years, who had never travelled on the philosophical grounds summed up as 'why run in the rain, it's as wet further on as it is here', decided to visit New Zealand to view the scenery she had seen pictures of. She was not disappointed, she pronounced it magnificent, and could not say enough good for the natural food there. She said that now she would die complete, having overcome what was, after all, a prejudice. The Pollyanna Enzyme was far-reaching. All political centres were closed. All armed forces were disbanded, which upset the major but what else could be done? No military were needed either to win wars or to control looting and rioting. The crime rate seemed to be about nil. Many people expected the usual effects of major crisis but the rules did not hold out when it was the End of Everything. The human mind had found new parameters which were at the same time much wider, and extremely narrow, so that people felt both free and secure at once, a unique state to be in. Few bothered to stop and bemoan the fact that this bliss was short-lived; it seemed acceptable and obvious that bliss is of its nature short-lived – anything longer is play acting bliss, and how the soul loathes that!

And as for animals and plants, if they knew what was coming, they didn't let on.

It was what prophets had loved to prophesy. Old Mother Shipton's Cave up in Yorkshire, England, was doing a roaring trade. She had prophesied the end of the the world – what did it matter that she was a little out in her dates? Well, seven hundred years, more or less. Fan Gleason, lovingly attended by Joe Sainsbury, who was painting a portrait of her with her strange new crooked smile, said that when she had been to Old Mother Shipton's Cave she had laughed at the prophecy. It just went to show.

It was officially announced by the World Health Bureau that there was no living thing on the planet which had escaped the attentions of the enzyme. At the buildings they paused in their celebrations, much as elsewhere, and said 'tell us something we don't know'. Some joker leapt onto a table and called out 'Yes folks, it's Doomsday' and a great series of cheers went up, more beer was fetched. It was suggested that they might barbecue an ox, if anyone could be bothered to go out and slaughter an ox – if they had the heart to do so. Maybe there would be a barbecue.

And the academics went on chuntering with their chicken and egg, was it inevitably affecting emotional response or was it a biochemical change in brain chemistry? It could have gone on for years, had there been time.

There were lulls in the party at the building from time to time for cleaning up and fetching supplies, and it was during one of these that Nurse Weldon, approximately one week away from zero, decided to return to the hospital where she had worked to look for a boyfriend she had there. On night duty they had spent some very pleasant time together and she missed him.

As she left, she passed the painter and his model, for they had set up in public as part of the general entertainment. It was a very lifelike portrait of the woman with her face twisted as if struck by lightning. It would have been possible to put it right but they preferred not to. The painter relished the beauty within the grotesque, and his sitter had no vanity remaining. Nurse Weldon went to the hospital, and it was there that she came across a secret.

Painter and model chatted as he worked.

'If only the plants could live and we could go, what a wonderful place this would be.'

'Yes, but if we were not there to admire it, would it exist?'

'That's philosophy, that is.'

'Still though, would it exist? I mean, how could it be proved?' They asked Pearl Weldon just as she was leaving, and she said she would think about it and tell them later. She mentioned it to the janitor at the hospital. She thought they would behave badly, like cannibals, pinching territory, strangling each other's growth. The janitor thought plants already had a consciousness.

'You only have to see the way my spider plant says good morning to me.'

'Oh, and how long has it been doing this?'

'Only a couple of weeks. Before that it was really surly. Now it reaches out its leaves.'

'Well now, isn't that nice?' Still, it wouldn't do that for much longer, she thought almost spitefully. He was crackers, that was his trouble – but he wasn't harming anyone. Everyone was doomed to die, what did one little loony matter? And then she discovered that maybe doom was not inevitable after all. Her friend was working on the problem day and night. He should not have told her, of course, but he did. Perhaps his subconscious wanted everyone to know – and he knew she would pass it on.

Back at the buildings she couldn't wait to talk about it even though it was against the Official Secrets Act. Such things now held no awe.

She told several people who were understandably as excited as she was.

One man. A Frenchman. Total immunity. Not a trace of it anywhere in him, and when they introduce it into his system it disappears. They are extremely short of time for research, of course, but there is an outside chance that they might produce an anti-toxin in time. The Frenchman himself did not know why he was being held.

'M'sieu, I am a free man, you 'ave no right to 'old me like this.'

'Yes we flippin' 'ave, mate. And we will. 'old out yer arms, I need more blood samples.'

'Ow. I will 'ave no blood left. What of my wife and family, I wish to join them. Everyone else is enjoying themselves but I am 'eld 'ere, why is this?'

'I can't tell you, keep still.' Everyone at the buildings wanted to know what was so special about a Frenchman.

'It's only one man, his nationality has nothing to do with it stupid. It's something in his blood, I don't honestly know, do I?'

'Blimey, he's worth a fortune and he doesn't know it. He could sell himself to science!'

'Mercenary so and so, such a thing is not to sell, it is for the benefit of humanity. Do you realise, he could be the man who could save the world?'

'Blimey.' They were rendered speechless.

'But M'sieu, I beg of you . . . ow . . . no more blood, I beg. I wish to return 'ome. What is for *déjeuner*, I am 'ungry, my wife will be cooking at this time . . .'

They told him that he could order whatever he liked, and they would get it for him perfectly cooked. They would get a special chef. And that was curiously appropriate, because the next morning a group of anarchists broke in, kidnapped him, took him into the yard and shot him dead. They felt they had rid the world of him, if he 'saved' it, how could it be good to live in any more after the last few weeks. There are some things that the human mind cannot digest. They set fire to the lab just in case there was sufficient research already done. A howl of dismay from the biochemists indicated that it might have been nearing completion, their precious research.

When this latest development reached the buildings, they rushed into the street cheering and they played music and danced. Nobody seemed to mind the death of the last hope. They hadn't wanted hope anyway. Hope has always been exhausting at the best of times.

The sun shone and the poisoned breeze blew gently. A perfect Spring day in which any Pollyanna could function perfectly. A chef absorbed in his craft announced that lunch for the imprisoned Frenchman was ready and could be taken immediately. Nobody had the heart to tell him the truth, so they took the splendid meal and gave it to the assassins, who had become heroes. Everybody was happy again. People chatting, being friends, playing. All was well. What they had got was exactly what they wanted – for the very first, and last time.

JOSEPHINE SAXTON
QUEEN OF THE STATES

'If you would like to dance hand in hand with a delightfully sympathetic, mad – or perhaps totally not mad – companion, this is your book. Highly recommended, especially to gourmets' Naomi Mitchison

Magdalen is on her own planet and out to lunch, weaving through the fantasies of those around her. She moves through time and space, from a private mental hospital to an alien spaceship where she is interrogated about the function of human sexual behaviour.

Is Magdalen mad, or have the aliens really landed? A brilliant original novel from this well known and loved British science fiction writer, author of *The Power of Time* (short stories, 1985) and four previous SF novels including *The Travails of Jane Saint and Other Stories* (The Women's Press, 1986).

0 7043 3992 7
£1.95

JOANNA RUSS
THE FEMALE MAN

'A visionary novel about a society where women can do all we now fantasize in closets and kitchens and beds ... intricate, witty, furious, savage' Marge Piercy

'A sophisticated work' *Sunday Times*

'A book women can read with glee' *City Limits*

The Female Man extends the boundaries of science fiction. It explores language and sexuality, customs and conventions, dreams and nightmares. It provides a witty and subversive analysis of the power men hold over women in our society.

sf

0 7043 3949 8
£1.95

THE ADVENTURES OF ALYX

Alyx – assassin, thief, hired bodyguard
Alyx – courageous, cunning and loyal to her own interests
Alyx – professional picklock, dragonslayer and wit
Alyx – 'among the wisest of a sex that is surpassingly wise'

The Adventures of Alyx are witty, serious, entertaining and profound. Alyx is a heroine beyond our wildest dreams.

sf

0 7043 3972 2
£1.95